A CLOSE CONNECTION

A CLOSE CONNECTION

PATRICIA FAWCETT

ROBERT HALE · LONDON

ISBN 978-0-7198-1447-1

Robert Hale Limited
Clerkenwell House
Clerkenwell Green
London EC1R 0HT

www.halebooks.com

2 4 6 8 10 9 7 5 3 1

Typeset in Palatino
Printed in Great Britain by Berforts Information Press Ltd.

To Chris at Buckland. With thanks for the first idea.

Chapter One

THE TAXI – or the luxury limousine as she preferred to think of it – was late. It had not been a good start to the day because Eleanor Nightingale could not get her suitcase zipped up, but even though it meant discarding that pair of high-heeled shoes that would have gone beautifully with her blue dress, it was finally done and the suitcase was sitting in the hall together with the others.

'Why did you leave it to the last minute?' her husband Henry asked as, ready now for the off, they hung about, glancing at their watches as the minutes ticked by. 'You've had enough practice at packing. You should have it off to a fine art by now.'

'Where is this driver? Five more minutes and I shall ring that office and give them what for.' Eleanor gave her husband an irritated look. 'You know nothing about packing at all. There's always something you have to put in at the very last minute. Anyway, this time it's different and I've not been able to concentrate properly. This time Paula and Alan are coming with us.'

'I don't see what difference that makes. It's your fault they're coming. There was no need for it. We don't have to be joined at the hip just because their son married our daughter.'

'Don't start on that again.'

'It's true. We haven't a thing in common apart from that and I warn you it's not going to be easy. I don't know what the hell you and Paula will find to talk about unless it's reality television. She seems to be an authority on that.'

'Don't be mean. We'll find something.' She smiled a little. 'Same for you, I suppose. What will you talk about with Alan?'

'God only knows but then we men don't talk like you ladies do.'

'I beg your pardon?'

'You know exactly what I mean. We don't go all emotional and start blubbing at the drop of a hat.'

'I don't blub.'

'You don't but Paula always looks as if she's on the brink. Haven't you noticed? I just hope it doesn't spoil the holiday, that's all, and for Christ's sake don't keep rubbing their noses in it that we have a hell of a lot more than they have. It's embarrassing.'

'As if I would do something like that.' Eleanor clicked her tongue. 'You know me better than that. I wouldn't dream of upsetting Paula. She's such a sweetheart.'

'Wouldn't you?' He eyed her with suspicion. 'Let's get one thing clear, my darling. Don't expect me to pay for everything. Let Alan dip into his pocket because that's what he will want to do. Give the guy some credit. I know they wanted to chip in with the wedding costs but you said no.'

'I made a decision I knew you wouldn't disagree with.'

'It would have been nice to be asked.'

'Don't be so touchy and you know you don't like to be bothered with trivialities.' She glanced once more at her watch. She hated being late for anything. She had arrived in this world three weeks early and that pretty much set the standard thereafter. 'It's a well-known fact that the bride's parents pay for their daughter's wedding especially if it is their precious

8

only daughter. It would have looked mean beyond belief if we had accepted the Walkers' offer. You know it was only a token offer. They never expected us to accept it in a million years.'

'I don't know about that. Times have changed.'

'What would you know about it?'

'Not much, I grant you, but I read somewhere that because couples normally live together beforehand they usually fork out for it themselves these days.'

'I can't think where you read that and may I remind you that Nicola and Matthew did not live together, strange as it might seem. I think it was so refreshing of them to wait until they were married before they set up home together.'

'I have a bad feeling about all this, this bloody holiday. And I don't feel that great either.' He rubbed ruefully at his stomach.

'We should have eaten.' Eleanor sighed. She rarely ate breakfast but Henry had eaten nothing either this morning, not able to face anything at this hour, and perhaps it was this that was making him irritable. He liked his food, did Henry, but he never gained an ounce. Luckily nor did she although she was considerably more careful about her diet.

'I just hope we get through this fortnight without a major row,' he went on, causing her to frown with exasperation. What was the matter with him this morning? He was in a singularly bad mood.

Minutes were ticking by and where on earth was this driver? They had used this company before, frequently, and they were usually so reliable. She hoped they were not becoming complacent, because there was more than one high-end taxi firm in the area and she did not feel a particular loyalty to this one.

'Why should there be a major row?' she asked, Henry's words prodding at her. 'You are such a pessimist. The Walkers are not like you, always flying off at the deep end for the slightest thing.'

'It's living with you that does it.' He grinned in that attractive way of his and against her better judgement she managed a small smile. 'You'd drive anybody bonkers, my darling. Being married to a practically perfect woman is very wearing.'

She ignored that. 'There won't be any rows. Paula is quite a timid sort and Alan is much more laid back. I've never heard him swear either so do try to moderate your language and not curse all over the place. I suppose he has to keep calm in his job. It wouldn't do if he got into a panic, would it?'

Henry grunted but said nothing.

For a moment she thought of Alan, a quiet thoughtful man whom she would like to get to know better. Of the two of them, Paula and Alan, she much preferred Alan but then she had never considered herself to be a woman's woman. She was much more at home with the men. Her darling son-in-law Matthew favoured his father in looks and temperament. 'The four of us are going to have a lovely time and there is so much I want to show Paula. Italy will be a completely new experience for her and she will love it. I can't believe she's never been to Europe.'

'All right.' He raised his hands in mock surrender. 'On your head be it.'

The bickering was nothing new but the taxi drew to a halt outside just then. It was too early in the day for an argument so she let it go, slinging her madly expensive handbag over her shoulder and leaving him and the driver to stuff the suitcases in the boot. Even though it would be quiet at this time of day, it would take some considerable time to get to the airport at Bristol and they needed to get going.

'You are very nearly fifteen minutes late,' she told the driver as she climbed in, shooting a glance at Henry that said clearly that on no account was he to tip him with his usual extravagance. He was not the normal driver which was just as well because the normal one was getting much too familiar.

'Sorry, my lovely,' the driver said, seemingly unperturbed but nevertheless setting off down the winding drive of their house at a fair speed, giving Eleanor no time for a last fond look at the house she loved, the house she would not be seeing for two whole weeks. 'Don't you fret. I'll get you there in time,' he said cheerfully, pausing before he exited the gates onto the lane.

'You'd better,' she retorted with a sniff. The familiarity of the 'my lovely' offended her but that was the Cornish for you and she had grown used to it. This part of the world seemed to operate on a different timescale and although the leisurely pace was quaint sometimes, it could be a huge irritation too.

'I feel a bit mean. We could have picked the Walkers up,' Henry muttered for her ears only, as they headed for the main road. 'It isn't much out of the way.'

'It's a lot out of the way,' she said. 'I hate the route over the Tamar Bridge and Paula was fine about it. In fact she insisted that they didn't want picking up.'

'She would say that. She hates to make a fuss. Haven't you noticed that either?'

'She seems to have made quite an impression on you.'

'I can sum people up pretty quickly. I got the measure of our Paula straight off. You're not jealous, are you?'

'Of Paula?' She laughed because she had also summed up the lady in question pretty quickly. She always went with her first impression for it usually proved to be right. A little lady, class-conscious and awkward, that was Paula. 'Why on earth would I be jealous of Paula?'

'How are they getting to the airport?'

'They are getting a lift from Eddie.'

'Who the hell is he?'

'A friend of Alan's. He's ex-navy.'

'Everybody's ex-navy in Plymouth.'

'Alan isn't.'

Eleanor adjusted her seatbelt, hoping they got there in time for a leisurely check-in because they were cutting it fine. She hoped to goodness that Paula and Alan were not there before them because they were not used to airports and they might start panicking, or at least Paula would. Paula was the queen of panic. She recalled the first time the Walkers had visited their house and the startled look on Paula's face.

Their house was situated halfway between the old Cornish capital of Launceston and the charming coastal resort of Bude and it was grand of course but it was not that grand, not by country-house standards – modest in fact – although she supposed in Paula's eyes it was practically in the stately-home category. To add to that perception, the day they visited would be when the gardener was out in the garden and the cleaner was pottering about indoors. Employing staff had very nearly caused Paula's eyes to pop out of their sockets.

'Sorry but it's the butler's day off,' Henry had joked, seeing the woman's face, and Paula had nodded earnestly, not getting the joke, until Alan laughed. Paula blushed then very nearly to the roots of her blonde hair, and Eleanor knew at that point that it was a waste of time, that she and Paula would never become true friends; the gap, that important social gap, was just too wide. It was a pity because she was short on proper friends, true friends, ladies on whom she could unload some of her problems and in turn listen sympathetically to theirs. She had loads of acquaintances and colleagues on the various committees of the various charitable organizations that she was part of, but no real friends. There was nobody she really trusted.

Why on earth had she done this? Why was she paying for this holiday for Nicola's in-laws? Sometimes she was surprised by her own generosity although it did no harm to be seen to be generous. She regretted the invitation as soon as she uttered it but even though Paula had seemed taken aback she said yes straightaway, although Eleanor could imagine the conversation she had with Alan once she got home. He was a proud man and he must have taken some persuading to agree to it.

'I think you are making a big mistake. Paula and Alan don't expect to be bosom friends with you,' her daughter had said, echoing what Henry was saying. 'I don't mean you should be enemies but it might be best to keep a distance. And to be honest, Mum, they'll just feel uncomfortable being on holiday with you. They're not like Matthew. You know him, he is so confident and he feels at home with anybody but they will just feel out of their depth on your sort of holiday. It's not fair to inflict it on them.'

Eleanor laughed at that. 'Inflict? I'm giving them a freebie, darling, and it isn't as if this is one of our special long-haul trips. It's relatively inexpensive. We can relax on holiday and it's time we got to know each other a bit more.'

'I don't see why. It will only lead to trouble and poor Paula will have to spend a fortune on clothes to keep up with you. She can't afford to spend a couple of hundred on a dress just because it takes her fancy and then stick it in the wardrobe and never ever wear it.'

'We all make wardrobe mistakes, darling. Even you. You are such a snob.' It surprised Eleanor that Nicola dismissed her in-laws in this way. They might be a little lower on the social ladder, certainly not the sort of people she normally associated with, but they were Matthew's parents and she liked Matthew very much and she wanted to get to know his parents, particularly his mother, a little more. After all, they had produced this marvellous son who was making her daughter so happy so there had to be something about them. Also, in due course, they would be grandparents together and it would be lovely if the new member of the family, even if he would be a Walker, was welcomed by both sets although, as she was Nicola's mother, she saw that she would have to take the upper hand as, being the maternal grandmother, she would take precedence.

Nicola and Matthew's house, the one they moved into after the wedding, was a disappointing choice; just a small, rather run-down cottage and she hoped that by the time a child arrived they would move to something more substantial, more in keeping with their position. By that time, Matthew could maybe think of starting up his own architectural practice specializing as he did in listed buildings and barn conversions which were prolific in the area, and he could do that from somewhere more central like Truro or maybe work from home which was much more feasible these days. He would do well in business because he was not short on confidence nor on charm and that was what endeared him to her, for she really could not be bothered with ditherers and dawdlers.

Henry dozed off on the journey to the airport but then they had been up much earlier than usual and he was not a morning person at the best of times. Henry had to ease himself into the day. At one time that involved a lot of cigarettes and coffee but thankfully he had given up the cigarettes.

In his mid-fifties now, he was aging rather well and looked handsome even when he was sleeping; such a strong face, a powerful man both in frame and personality. Henry Nightingale was the sort of man who lit up a room and it was small wonder that he was successful in business because he looked dependable, confident and self-assured, the sort of man you could trust, and it was the power that he wielded even when younger that had attracted her to him. Looking back, she was very young when they met, barely twenty-four, but according to her mother, time was already passing her by and she was in danger of leaving it a little late.

'Before you know it, you will be thirty,' that lady said. 'And all the best ones will have been snapped up and you will be left with the dregs.'

'I have a career, Mummy,' she told her. 'I'm really not that interested in getting married.'

'You say that now but believe me it will be a different story in a few years and you need to get one baby under your belt before you start panicking about it.'

'I'm not entirely sure I want a baby either. I'm not that maternal.'

'None of us are until we have a child.' That was rich coming from Mummy, who had never been what they now call 'hands-on'.

However, about that time Eleanor's friends were beginning to become attached and the engagement announcements were starting to appear and, after being bridesmaid at various weddings, she was suddenly feeling left out.

She wanted a man of her own.

Henry's arrival home from some time spent in London was a godsend with her mother, a keen reader of Jane Austen novels, taking on the role of a present-day Mrs Bennet in full matchmaking mode.

It was to be an odd relationship in those early days, too measured to be in any way spontaneous, but on the plus side they made an attractive couple and that pleased Henry. There was no spark between them, sadly, but weighing up the pros and cons he did not fare too badly. He was from a West Country family as well connected as hers, in addition acquiring a substantial sum of money of his own from an aunt who had adored him. He was built in the manner of a rugby player with a grace that belied his size and Eleanor, tall for a girl, needed a man of height.

However, there had to be more to it than looks. Eleanor, aided by her mother, who had a first-class degree in devious enquiries, made sure that he was sound before she allowed their relationship to proceed, for she had determined at an early age that she was not going to go through life counting pennies. Marrying below never worked, her mother said.

If Henry had been lacking in financial terms then she – or

more likely her formidable mother – would have instantly put an end to it before it escalated. In the event, once she decided he was the one for her, she kept him at arm's length for some considerable time to make sure that his appetite was whetted. She only agreed to full-on lovemaking once there was an agreeably large diamond ring on her finger with the wedding date fixed. She supposed she was old-fashioned in that she had only limited sexual experience prior to Henry and perhaps that was why she had always been faintly disappointed in that aspect of their life, although she never let on to him. Henry had an outrageous overconfidence about his sexual ability; he was robust certainly but it was all about him and his needs and he was lacking in anything resembling gentleness, which she craved. She was never quite sure why he married her for there was a string of girlfriends before her, although perhaps his own mother was tiring of his bachelor ways and had a hand in it. He said he loved her and perhaps he did but his roving eye was a problem from the honeymoon onward.

Love at first sight was a myth perpetrated by romantic novelists and she had never given any credence to it. A successful marriage could be achieved through hard work and a certain give and take, and over the years she had learned how to handle Henry. She was the boss at home and, when it came to domestic matters, he could be persuaded at every turn to agree to what she decided. She had issued the invitation to Paula and Alan without consulting Henry and, as expected, he had agreed to it, albeit with reservations.

He would be proved wrong for she felt in her bones that this holiday would be an unqualified success.

Once they got up in the air, that is, if the wretched driver ever got them there on time. She would complain to the company when they got back. She was tempted to nudge Henry awake but they had a way to go yet and he could be very grumpy if his sleep was unnaturally curtailed.

How could he fall asleep under such conditions as this? Eleanor felt more excited than tired at the prospect of being back in Italy, which was by far her favourite country. They had travelled extensively, done most of the world apart from the Indian continent, which she simply did not fancy, or the cold trips up to the Arctic and so on. They could keep those kind of holidays, thank you very much.

She had slept badly too, childishly excited on the holiday eve, although she could not drop off as easily as Henry, finding it impossible to relax when the driver clearly thought his driving was Grand Prix standard.

Once they were safely on the motorway, he made a brief attempt to engage her in conversation, but she cut him short for at this unearthly hour she was in no mood for it, and he quickly stopped trying. She needed him to concentrate on what he was doing. As a careful driver herself, she had a horror of being a passenger and at times she had to close her eyes as he hurtled along far too fast in the outside lane of the M5.

All she wanted was for him to get them to the airport in one piece on time.

Chapter Two

PAULA WALKER HAD no trouble fastening her suitcase, but once it was done she worried that the cases looked shabby and she wished she had bought new ones as she had wanted to do, before her son convinced her that it was not a problem. He had popped over to see them last Sunday, pleasing her with the impromptu visit, although he had insisted on taking them out for lunch at some posh hotel when she would rather have cooked him a proper roast dinner instead.

The hotel was out in the country, on Dartmoor, but not the one Nicola worked at. She was on weekend duty which explained why he was alone.

'She's fine, thanks,' Matthew said when she enquired after her. 'Rushed off her feet of course. They are very busy with wedding receptions. Why does everybody want to get married in June?'

'Your mum and I got married in June,' Alan said with a smile. 'Remember that, sweetheart?'

'Of course I do.' She gave him a fond glance before looking at her son, who was watching the pair of them with a silly grin on his face. She hoped to goodness his marriage would prove to be as happy as theirs but it was not the sort of thing you could ask about. She hoped her womanly intuition was wrong, but she had always harboured a slight doubt about the speed of it all. It wasn't as if there was a reason for it because Nicola was not pregnant, not that that sort of thing mattered these days. These days, as often as not, the couple's children were at the wedding.

Things had come a long way and she wasn't sure whether or not it was for the best, but there it was and you couldn't change it. Just like there was no way they could go back to being without the Internet or mobile phones. They were here to stay. Even in this restaurant they had been interrupted once or twice by somebody's phone going off. She kept her thoughts to herself though, because she did not want anybody accusing her of being a grumpy old woman. She was not grumpy, not often, and she certainly was not old.

Matthew had had a few girlfriends over the years since he left university but none of them were particularly serious. It never occurred to her when he brought Nicola home to see them that there was anything special about the girl, or that it would be anything other than casual, petering out eventually as the others had. To her, he had never quite got over losing his first love who had upped and left the area – and him – just before he went off to university. It hit him badly even though it would never have lasted in any case and then shortly afterwards they lost Lucy too so it was a double whammy for Matthew.

Nicola, cool-eyed and a little aloof, was different from the others. Her first impression of the girl was mixed. She tried to like her for obvious reasons but it did not quite work that way. Worryingly, she liked Nicola a lot less than she had liked some of the others but she had no option but to make the best of it. Nicola was a little too brisk for her liking, too superficial with her perfect make-up and immaculate clothes and, right from the off, she had the uncomfortable feeling that she was looking down at her, sometimes annoyingly talking to her as if she did not possess a single brain cell.

'Give the girl a chance,' Alan said when she told him about her doubts. 'I know she's a bit on the posh side but we shouldn't hold that against her. She can't help that, can she?'

No, of course not, but the doubts persisted.

She knew she was guilty of making snap judgements about people, not always getting it right and so she had to hope that on this occasion she was wrong and that her feelings would mellow and that, in due course, certainly before a baby appeared on the scene, she and her daughter-in-law might become friends of a sort.

She knew she had a tendency to overreact and dwell on anything associated with class and she had to remember that Nicola was her son's choice so she must keep quiet. Even so, she still felt awkward in Nicola's company and was happier when Matthew came to visit on his own and, on this occasion, this Sunday surprise was a delight. Matthew drove them out to the hotel with his father just about managing to avoid a negative comment about the driving because, up on the moor, you had to watch out for wandering sheep and ponies and cattle. They could appear out of nowhere with a surprising turn of speed at that and the thought of accidentally hitting one of them was something she dare not contemplate.

At the hotel, Matthew slotted the car into a space and they stepped out into the warm sunshine. She had not been here before and it looked lovely, although she wondered if her hastily put-on smart dress was smart enough. But Matthew had whisked them here and she hadn't had time to think too much about what to wear. They did bar meals but Matthew had booked them into the dining room and she followed him to their table by the window, inadvertently depriving the hovering waiter of pulling out her chair by doing it herself. She did not care for all this palaver as with elaborate movements the waiter took the napkin off the table and placed it reverently on her lap. Opposite her, Alan raised his eyebrows, which nearly set her off. She had a tendency to giggle at inappropriate moments and this was one of them. She knew she had better not catch his eye again whilst the waiter was in spectacular fussy attendance.

'This is very nice,' she said as they waited for their meal to arrive. This hotel didn't do a carvery, which she preferred, and it was all a bit too starchy for her with an icy atmosphere you could cut with one of the heavy silver knives, and whispered conversations all around, but she determined to make the best of it with Matthew insisting that they had the lot: starter, main and dessert. It was his treat and he wouldn't even let his father pay for the drinks.

The starters, bits and bobs of this and that, were served on tiny pieces of slate and she saw the look Alan gave them, heard the whisper to Matthew that if he wanted his dinner served on a slate he would have got the ladder up and pinched one from the roof.

'Go with it, Dad,' Matthew said. 'It's the new presentation and it's all the rage these days. Wait until you get to Italy. It'll be Italian food there.'

'Don't be cheeky.' Much more at ease than she was in any situation, Alan pretended to cuff his son, the family resemblance clearly visible. They were a good-looking lot, the Walkers, and for a moment she looked on proudly. 'I can't wait to see Venice and Verona. I've read up on Venice and I'm awash with information,' he added with a big grin.

Matthew laughed. 'Trust you. You'll know exactly what you want to see, then?'

'You bet. I have it all worked out. I can't wait but your mum's getting in a bit of a state though. Aren't you, Paula?'

'Why?' Matthew looked at her. He was wearing jeans of all things, jeans at this hotel, but with a linen jacket and open-necked shirt. It was a young man's look and at least the jeans were in one piece and not fashionably ripped at the knees.

Next to him, in his grey suit with a neatly knotted tie, Alan looked quite middle-aged. 'What's there to get in a state about, Mum?'

She mentioned the sad condition of their luggage then. She had bought some new clothes for the trip, absolute necessities, but she had spent quite a bit, and she couldn't in all honesty run to a new set of suitcases as well. They had had them forever and although they were rarely used they were cheap to start off with and had not stood up well to the test of time. They looked shabby and she would be ashamed dragging them off the carousel at the airport.

'Not a problem. You should see the sort of bags well-travelled people have,' Matthew said. 'Battered and falling to bits, the more bashed up the better.'

Paula looked at him, puzzled, but then Matthew often puzzled her these days. 'We're not well travelled,' she said stiffly.

'Mum, you are worrying about nothing. They're absolutely fine. You can borrow some from us if you like. I'll mention it to Nicola.'

'No,' she said hastily because she did not want Nicola knowing and saying something to Eleanor. 'We'll make do with what we have.'

Even so …

She sat in the living room of her terraced house in Plymouth waiting for Eddie to arrive to take them to the airport. He had offered, so they had taken him up on it, although Alan thought that the Nightingales might have suggested they share the luxury limousine that was taking them. It wasn't much of a detour to pick them up on their way from Cornwall if they came via the Tamar Bridge, but she thought that the offer Eleanor made was half-hearted and she hadn't wanted to put them out any more than they were doing already. After all, this holiday wasn't costing them a penny other than the petrol money they would pay Eddie and a few spends, not to mention the clothes-buying, of course, which she was keeping quiet about. She did not tell Alan everything and she suspected he kept a few things from her as well.

Eddie was notoriously late for everything though, and she wished now that they had arranged an alternative means of transport or they could have taken the car and left it parked at the airport, but Alan had said no to that.

Their flight was later in the morning, but they had to be at the airport for check-in hours earlier and it was a bit of a trek up the M5 to Bristol. Even though they had not felt like it, she had made them a cooked breakfast because heaven only knows when they would eat next and it was common knowledge that the aeroplane food was rubbish. She was also not entirely sure that, rubbish or not, she would be able to eat anything up in the air like that. She had been on a plane, once, just a short trip just after she and Alan got married, and she had not liked it particularly but she was keeping her nerves in check because she did not want Her Ladyship to catch on that she was jittery.

The Nightingales had travelled to practically every corner of the globe as Eleanor had been keen to tell her. This little jaunt to Italy was the third holiday so far this year as they had already been on a city break to Paris and a Caribbean cruise.

All right for some.

She tried not to let it get to her because jealousy was an ugly emotion, but meeting Eleanor and Henry for the first time had been an eye-opener. Talk about how the other half live and that kitchen of hers had more gadgets than the Lakeland catalogue. It all seemed effortless for the Nightingales, both of whom had been born with a silver spoon in their mouths. Nicola was the only child at that and maybe that explained it. Nicola was used to getting what she wanted, used to getting her own way, used to people giving in to her, and Matthew seemed content to let her have what she wanted. She wanted that cottage, for instance, when she knew Matthew had serious doubts about its condition. Roses around the door and ivy and other climbing stuff could hide a multitude of sins and there was the problem of damp with it being so close to the river, not to mention the tricky access up that narrow lane, but there was no way Nicola would be persuaded out of it once she had made up her mind. Matthew had gone along with it, but in Paula's eyes he should have put his foot down.

'Have you got the passports?' she asked Alan for the umpteenth time and he nodded, patting the pocket of his jacket.

Alice, next door, had a key and she would pop in and pick up the post and make sure that the newsagent had got the message and cancelled the papers. She did not want a heap of papers and her magazines lying in the hall when they got back. There was nothing in the fridge and everything was switched off, but it was worrying her a bit because they had never been away for more than a week in their lives, and they were going to be in Italy for just over a fortnight. Fifteen days, that was what it said in the brochure, the brochure she had looked at over and over again ever since Eleanor had given it to her. The hotel looked fabulous, shining in the sunshine with its gardens and its pool and opposite it the lake was so blue.

Alan had been doing some research, poring over books for weeks now, reading up on the area they would be visiting because he liked to do his homework and he loved maps and map-reading. He had pointed out to her various places he wanted to see, but as she reminded him it was up to Eleanor and Henry as they would have to stick together or it would look rude.

'Where has Eddie got to?' Alan said, opening the front door and peering down the street as if that would make him come any quicker. The street sloped at a terrifying angle but then most of the streets round here did the same, and Eddie might be finding it hard to find a place to park. She hoped they wouldn't have to drag the cases up or down the street. Last winter, during an icy spell, it had been like stepping out onto a ski slope. She was terrified she might come a cropper and break her ankle just like a woman at work had done, although she had been in Switzerland at the time, which made it a bit more romantic – although just as painful.

'I wouldn't care if I'd been off-piste,' the girl told them when she got back, hobbling about in plaster, milking it for all it was worth and messing up their rota for weeks because she reckoned she could only stand for ten minutes at a time. 'But I just fell over in the street when we were on our way to the ski-lifts and I heard it crack. I said to him, I've broken my bloody ankle and he just laughed.'

'Off-piste means a slope where beginners shouldn't really be,' somebody else had said, looking at Paula in kindly explanation, when in fact she knew exactly what was meant. People were forever doing that to her. Did she look like she was stupid?

It was early morning, chilly with the door open but dry and light already even at this hour and, according to the weather forecast, the clouds would lift later and, once they got to Italy, it promised to be sunshine all the way. The sun cream was in the bag as well as a sun hat, a cream, big-brimmed straw decorated with pink beading that she had picked up last week. She was not going to tell a soul but she had bought it from the children's section at Debenhams; it fitted her perfectly so what did it matter if it said 9-10 years on the label? The adult hats had swamped her.

Paula stood up, hitching up her trousers. Travel light, Matthew had said, and she was doing that. These trousers were being a blessed nuisance because, even though she had taken up the hem – she always had to take up hems – she had misjudged it and they were still a fraction long and would be fraying before long. Cream straight-leg trousers, white tee-shirt and a cotton jacket, all from the mail order catalogue that had a better-than-average petite section, even though it wasn't quite petite enough. Wedge heels to give her some much-needed height and she was ready for the off. Had been ready for the off for hours now. There had been two visits to the loo already and if Eddie didn't get here soon she would have to pay a further visit. Excitement always affected her bladder.

She wondered what on earth Eleanor would be wearing. If the wedding was anything to go by, it would be something expensive and exclusive, but then Eleanor was lucky: she had a model figure, tall and slim and impossibly elegant with luxuriant dark-brown hair the envy of a woman half her age. Eleanor was a year older than she, but that was nothing when you looked as good as she did. Eleanor could, as they said, carry any look off whereas she had to be very careful that she didn't look frumpy. Not having a daughter to give her fashion advice was a disadvantage but they had lost their lovely Lucy when she was thirteen and she did not care to dwell on that.

'Here he is. About time.' Alan had the bags out on the street, as Eddie reversed smartly into a gap right outside their front door. He got out and slammed the door, in danger of waking up the whole street as he announced that his alarm had not gone off and that he still had his pyjama bottoms on under his trousers.

'Don't make such a racket, Eddie.' Paula shushed him, hearing every little sound magnified fifty times, glancing up anxiously at the curtained, darkened windows of the sur-rounding houses, as he and Alan got the bags into the boot and Eddie, oblivious, slammed all the doors shut, starting up the engine of the big old car with enough roaring revs to wake the dead.

Taking a final look at the street as they drove off, Paula wondered if she would ever set eyes on it again. In a short time, they would be up in the air on their way to Milan. Fifteen days was a long time and, as they turned the corner, she already felt a bit homesick.

Chapter Three

ABOUT THE SAME time as her parents and parents-in-law were boarding their flight, Nicola Walker was getting ready to go to work. She was late and she was very cross. She and Matthew had had words last thing and although they still slept together in their king-sized bed, it was an uncomfortable night, both of them sleeping on the edge. They had managed a goodnight kiss, as chill as a block of ice-cream, but since then had been careful not to fall into the middle of the bed where they would end up in a cosy warm heap. The so-called master bedroom in the cottage was tiny, not really big enough for the bed let alone any other piece of furniture and living in what felt like a doll's house was beginning to depress her more and more.

Out here in the back of beyond, it was pitch dark too when night came but uncannily not completely silent, with an owl hooting and hunting in the woods followed by a scary screech when it found its prey. The trees creaked and groaned, things – God knows what – scudded around in the bushes and what had once seemed such an idyllic home was now showing all its faults.

The roses round the door – yes, there really had been roses – and the pretty blossoms of the climbers that draped the outside wall disguised damaged brickwork that Matthew really ought to have picked up. But, on the day they viewed, the sun was shining, the whoosh of the river as it swooped down in a mini-waterfall just below the bridge was delightful, the cottage garden was a riot of colour and she was wearing rose-tinted spectacles. Matthew had been less than enthusiastic and it was she who had insisted that this was the house of their dreams so she supposed, in all fairness, she could not blame him entirely. She had seen the programmes on television where they did a complete makeover in a matter of weeks, the transformation miraculous, and here they were, a year on, and they were no nearer.

She wanted to move out of this hellhole as soon as possible. They had talked about it but they could not afford it as Matthew had tried patiently to explain to her, but she was not going to let a small matter of finance put her off. There had to be a way. There was always a way. Some of their friends earned less than they did and they had fancier homes. Matthew was unimpressed by that, saying that they were probably head over heels into debt but although he was right, in a way, she was not going to be put off.

She wanted something bigger and altogether grander with a large garden and a terrace where they could sit out and entertain in summer, something rather like her parents' house. She wanted her friends to ooh and aah about her home, to be jealous in fact. She wanted one of those gorgeous bright-blue Agas and a kitchen to die for instead of this cramped galley that would not be out of place on a narrowboat with their dining table in an alcove just off the kitchen so that your guests could see your every culinary move. She was a very messy cook and she did not want to be on show when she was working nor was it so easy to cheat with M&S ready meals when so many eyes were watching. So, in addition to the must-have list she had already compiled in her head, there must also be a separate grown-up dining room. She had seen the very table she wanted already, oval and glass-topped and a bit pricey at just over £2,000 for the table alone but it was modern and edgy and the chairs that accompanied it were bright blue. Her mother would think it ghastly but she wanted to get as far away as possible from the boring traditional.

After lying stiffly awake thinking about all this for what seemed hours, she finally drifted off to dream about it, only to wake early before the alarm went off and, with last night's heated words retreating into her sleepy morning head, she relented a little, rolling towards the middle of the bed. To her annoyance, Matthew pretended to be asleep when he plainly was not and she was hanged if she was going to make the first conciliatory move. She wanted an apology which she might just deign to accept if it was a genuine attempt on his part.

But none was forthcoming.

'Sod you, then,' she said, making a big deal of sitting up and reaching for her wrap and getting up, banging her toe in the process as she often did on the bedpost, letting out a curse and shutting her ears to what sounded suspiciously like a muffled laugh from her husband's apparently sleeping form.

Surprisingly it was their first major row and, up and about now down in the kitchen, it was stinging still, because, until you had a row with somebody, a proper one, you had no real idea how they would react, whether they would be steely-eyed and sullen or downright aggressive, giving as good as they got.

She had seen the latter reaction recently from a hotel guest who had quite simply 'lost it' and it had not been pleasant to see. On that occasion, the manager had to be called for and he had been his usual calm and controlled self, managing to calm the man down and offer an ingratiating and, in her eyes, humiliating apology which duly satisfied the guest.

Nicola knew she had not handled that situation well, in grave danger of losing it herself and telling the guy, hotel guest or not, where to put his complaint, a complaint that was in her eyes totally unjustified.

'Be careful, Nicola,' Gerry Gilbert had said, taking her aside and giving her a not very happy look when the guest had departed. 'I know that guests can be extremely difficult sometimes but you've got to learn not to react. You should know by now that one of the cardinal rules is never talk back.'

'I do know that but ...' She was very nearly guilty then of arguing with the manager himself which would have done her no favours whatsoever and, aware that she had earned a black mark, it put her in a rotten mood for the rest of the day.

But that guest had been a stranger, the row quickly forgotten, and having a good old row with someone you loved was all a bit different with a new dimension added. Her mother and father did not row as such, certainly not full-blown yelling matches, but as she grew up she was often aware of an atmosphere, a peculiar sort of silence, and she quickly learnt that she was best out of the way on occasions such as that until the whole thing, whatever it was, blew over. It wasn't until she was into her teens that she realized just what the silences had been about. It was a bitter blow too when she realized that her parents' marriage was far from perfect. Her mother suffered in silence and her father took her very much for granted.

She had just discovered that Matthew was impossible to argue with, not with any degree of satisfaction, because he simply would not retaliate, much too chilled-out. In some ways, a good old slanging match, quickly over, would have been easier to deal with but he remained irritatingly cool and unmoved, voice level, whilst she felt herself getting hot and bothered, heard her voice rising, which meant ultimately that she was losing the argument as he sat there with a bemused expression on his face, trying in vain to calm her down. She had called him names, which she now regretted because it was so childish and she had sworn a lot too which he did not care for, but then he could be annoyingly puritanical at times.

She could almost see herself, face contorted with anger, spitting out her words, flushed, with her eyes bulging, spittle escaping her mouth, a very bad look indeed so that, in the end, frustrated beyond belief that she was getting no reaction from him, she had no option but to storm out of the room and leave him to it. The sitting-room door was swollen with the heat and was sticking, at that, so it wasn't as if she could slam it with any satisfaction. If he expected her to dissolve into ladylike tears then he had another think coming. She prided herself on being able to contain tears as her mother did and she really had no time for 'weepers'. Weeping really was a very underhand way of trying to get what you want. Women who resorted to tears might actually get their way but they let the sisterhood down.

Now, remembering last night, she was sulking and Matthew, showered, shaved and dressed for work, was foolishly pretending that all was well, whistling as he made himself a full English breakfast, the complete cholesterol works, before sitting down opposite her. Sitting with her glass of orange juice and slice of toast thinly coated with some sort of disgusting good-for-you spread, she gave a disapproving sniff towards the bacon, sausage and egg on his plate but he took no notice.

It was hard work, however, sulking and although, just like her father, she did not think of herself as a morning person, she normally said *something* over breakfast. They always sat down at the table for they had agreed at the start of their marriage that they would try and sit down in a civilized manner to begin the day. Radio Two blared out a tune, something cheerful and completely inappropriate this morning, and at last she could stand it no longer. She was not a sulking sort; her temper flared and retreated as quickly as it came and even though she felt she was backing down she finally broke the silence.

'All right, babe, you win. But if you think I'm going to

apologize just because you overreacted, you can think again,' she began, knowing it was not the best opening, the prelude to another row if anything, but it was how she felt and he needed to know.

'Oh, come on, darling, let's not let this escalate any further,' he said, smiling his first smile of the day, boringly correct as usual for they needed to put this behind them, also boringly unmoved as if he could smile his way back into her affections. 'It was all heat-of-the-moment stuff and I forgive you,' he added rubbing salt into the wound because she knew in her heart that she was the one who had taken umbrage and turned what had merely started off as an observation into a row.

'You've got egg on your chin,' she said, frowning at him as he wiped his chin with a piece of kitchen roll. Even though she had been up early they were now close to running late and she glanced at the clock, a wedding present, a big faux station clock that hung importantly from a hook on the roughly plastered kitchen wall. 'Look at the time; we'd better get a move on.' She hesitated a moment and then went for it because it would bother her all day if they did not settle this. 'Although I honestly think you overreacted hugely, I didn't mean to imply that your mother was thick and I'm sorry if you thought that.'

He said nothing but his smile faltered.

'I didn't mean for a minute that Paula was thick,' she continued, pressing the point home. 'I just said that she would find it difficult on the holiday keeping up with my mother. Socially and intellectually they are poles apart.'

'There you go again. For goodness' sake, Nicola, I never realized you were such a snob.'

'You are so wrong there. And you can't face facts. I'm not making a public announcement, I'm just telling you. Mother was privately educated, went to university, got her degree, taught for several years and speaks fluent Italian for one thing and there's no surer way of feeling inferior than if you are standing beside somebody who speaks the language and you haven't a clue what's going on.'

'My mother may not have a degree—'

'She doesn't. And I didn't mean anything by that either. Lots of very successful people don't have degrees.' She did not bother to add, though, that his mother was hardly the success of the century. Her patience was wearing thin and she felt the first surge of another bout of anger which would be a bad start to the day. She really needed to calm herself down. 'Sorry,' she murmured, putting her hand over his. 'But you must not be so sensitive, sweetie. I like Paula. I like her a lot. She's very sweet-natured.'

He nodded, managing a rueful smile at that.

She could murder the woman, she thought later, on the drive to work. She had told a lie, a white one, back there because sweet-natured was not the first thing that came to mind when she thought about her dearest mother-in-law. Well, all right, she was sweet-natured in that she was the sort of agreeable woman who didn't have a bad word to say about anybody but that just made her boring as hell. Having an edge made people so much more interesting. Nicola liked people about whom you were never quite sure, people with a hint of mystery, maybe a dark side to them but she found open-natured people like dear Paula mildly irritating.

It was a complete surprise when they met. She had no idea what she had imagined, what sort of person she had conjured up in her mind but Paula was nothing like it. How on earth could such a sparrow-like nothing of a woman produce a son as dashing as Matthew?

Paula Walker was the sort of woman who made her cringe. She was too much of the little helpless woman, in every way, a bit wet, a bit inconsequential, the sort of woman who would be great as a film extra because she would not stand out in the crowd. And she wore such nondescript cheap clothes, the sort that made her shudder; although that was just a matter of poor taste and she could be helped with that if she wanted.

So her first impression of the woman who was to be her future mother-in-law was a big disappointment.

Sometimes women like her, the petite variety, were little fireballs as feisty as you come, but that was not Paula and the way she looked up to Alan with that adoring gaze was not far short of nauseating. Did the woman have no opinion of her own? Did she have to defer to her man for every damned thing? Her own mother had an opinion about everything, sticking to it at that, even if she was wildly off the mark as she frequently was, and she was sure that she had only voted Lib Dem at the last election because her father always voted Tory.

You could bet your life that Paula would vote the same way as her husband and worse, would not consider any-thing wrong with that. Nicola had no idea how Matthew voted although she could hazard a guess but, although they never argued about politics or religion – taboo subjects, both – she really didn't give a fly's fart about his political leanings because he would never influence her.

The two leading ladies in her life were so far removed from each other it was almost comic. Poor Paula would die a thou-sand deaths if her mother subjected her to dining out in any of the exclusive dining establishments the Nightingales fre-quented, where she insisted on the best wine and so on, her mother in particular making the poor maître d' work for his living. Matthew had told her about taking his parents out for lunch to a hotel over on Dartmoor and about how nervous his mother had been throughout, socially uncomfortable and not enjoying the 'ambience' one little bit, her anxiety managing to ruin things for him.

However, Nicola had learnt something last night. Matthew reacted badly to criticism of his mother, even if it was deserved, so for the sake of peace and harmony she would just have to button up in future. It was lovely in a way, for a son should stick up for his mother whatever the circumstances, but she suspected that, deep down, he might well agree with her and he probably felt guilty about that. Going to university, mixing with the Oxford set, had changed him and he had grown apart from his parents and their small lives. Within her own narrow world, Paula could hold her own, but step outside it and the poor soul was all a-flutter.

Nicola was glad, though, that she and Matthew had managed a quick kiss goodbye before she set off this morning and his murmured 'Don't let's argue again' had meant something. Maybe they would make up properly this evening and, as it was his turn to cook, she hoped he would get a bottle of wine even if it was midweek and they were trying to limit their drinking.

To her delight, her husband was the sort of man whom women inevitably stole a glance at and he was not even aware of his powers of attraction. There was no strutting around peacock-like from Matthew, just a slotting into whatever situation he happened to find himself. He was too fair-haired to fall into the tall, dark and handsome category, but there was just something about him, that indefinable something that ought to be snapped up and bottled.

She remembered clearly the first time she saw him at the hotel where he was attending some function, a boring-sounding seminar that had spilled over into the evening. The women in the group had abandoned their working suits and gone to town on their frocks as if it was some glitzy Christmas ball. The men were more soberly clad but even in the male uniform of well-tailored dark suit and white shirt, Matthew managed to stand out from the others.

By God, he looked good. She heard him laugh first and looked across, seeing some woman in a fitted red dress beside him, a little dark-haired woman with a big bust, unashamedly flirting with him. Really, must she make it quite so obvious? Matthew was being charming but not taking the bait and she smiled to herself that all that ridiculous pouting and eye-fluttering was coming to nothing.

It was Nicola's Mr Darcy moment, although she hoped as he glanced her way that she turned away before he detected her interest. She was supposed to be invisible, working at the time, assisting overseeing the corporate event and making sure it ran smoothly with no hitches, ready for action if it was necessary, standing unobtrusively off to one side watching proceedings in general but him in particular. She was not in the market for romance, for any sort of long-term thing, but not averse to a fling and there had been one or two of those at university and since, plus a few one-night stands at that, things she cringed at when she looked back at them.

She took after her mother with the same heavy dark hair and tall slender frame. She was not sure of her father's con-tribution to the gene pool but she supposed some aspect of her personality was gained from him, for her father possessed a natural aura of charm and confidence and an undoubted ability to attract the opposite sex. That night, the night she met Matthew, she was severely hampered by her neat but dull suit so she could not compete with the woman in the sexy red dress but thank goodness her make-up was spot on and her hair looked good swept up.

It was entirely unethical of course to approach him in any way but she must have made some impression for he approached her as the party dispersed, exchanging a few words and somehow in the process getting hold of her mobile number. He was utterly charming with a gorgeous smile that reached his eyes but afterwards she felt quite flustered at the prospect of him contacting her again. She did not normally hand out her personal number to strangers – let there be a modicum of holding back, for heaven's sake – but he seemed witty and warm and it was love at first sight even if her mother laughed at that and told her she was watching too many of those romantic comedies. Walking on air – well, it felt suspiciously like that – she wished then that she had mentioned her feelings because normally she and her mother pretty much avoided talking about such things.

'Love at first sight? Really, darling, I am sorry to disillusion you but it simply doesn't work like that,' her mother said. 'It takes years to learn to love a man and in the end it's more a case of just being used to each other and rather liking each other's company.'

'Thanks for that,' she said, amused and not entirely surprised by her mother's interpretation. She doubted her mother had ever been in love. She was in love with Matthew, never doubting for a minute that he was her Mr Right, and she was not going to let her mother's rather jaded ideas about that stop her from believing it.

Her parents, particularly her father, were surprised at their insistence on a short engagement but they liked Matthew – also at first sight – and he charmed them as he had charmed her. Their only doubt was that the two of them were young to be considering marriage in this day and age, thirty-two and twenty-nine respectively, but they had not a leg to stand on there for both sets of parents had married when they were much younger.

Paula had only been twenty-two when she had Matthew, a mere child, and her own mother only a little older so if she became pregnant tomorrow she would be older than they when she had her first child. They should be glad they had decided to get married rather than opting to live together for a few years before they committed to that.

Once the wedding date was settled, her mother pulled out all the stops, sadly spared the delights of the long-term planning she had been looking forward to, but managing, with Nicola's budding events expertise on hand, to arrange the whole caboodle within weeks. There were a few raised eyebrows, no doubt, at what seemed the unseemly rush. Nicola did wonder herself just why they were going the whole hog when they scarcely knew each other, when they had never actually lived together at that, but it seemed right and – what the hell – she had caught something of the bridal excitement as an events coordinator, her job being to make sure that their brides had a day to remember. And being the centre of attention, if only for one day, was not something to be sniffed at.

She had always told herself she would be married some day, preferably before she was an age when she would look ridiculous in a wedding gown, and now, nearing thirty, seemed as good a time as any. At thirty, she knew her own mind and it really did not concern her what other people might think. Her dress was slim and elegant, costing a bomb of course, although to keep the peace they halved the price when Father asked. He was practically a millionaire, for heaven's sake, wildly extravagant in some ways and brutally tight in others.

Despite the rushed-through arrangements, it was a fairy-tale wedding, no expense spared of course, their vows exchanged in the sweetest little village church imaginable, followed by a reception held in a marquee on the lawn at her parents' house. The honeymoon in the Maldives courtesy of her parents had been fabulous. She could not believe that she was Mrs Walker, married to this fabulous man. How lucky was she?

Then, it was home to the little cottage by the bridge, the boundary bridge that separated the counties of Devon and Cornwall, and indeed, the Welcome to Kernow sign was just a few hundred yards down the track from their cottage.

That cottage, Honeysuckle Cottage would you believe, that had seemed so cosy and romantic a year ago, was now, with its insufferably twee name, getting on her nerves big-time.

Chapter Four

SOMETIMES, KICKING UP a stink was the only way to deal with an awkward situation and Eleanor was fully prepared to do just that when she discovered that, of the two rooms allocated to them, only one had a lake view with balcony. The whole tour group had assembled in the spotlessly clean, flower-filled hotel foyer in order to collect their room keys and most of their party had already disappeared towards the lifts that would take them up to those rooms.

The four of them were left, tired and a little dishevelled, but it looked as if they would not be getting up to their rooms for a while yet, not until this was sorted to Eleanor's satisfaction.

'We don't mind, do we, Alan?' Paula said, a little tight-lipped as the tour representative was called over to the reception desk. Eleanor's conversation with the reception clerk had been conducted in Italian – even though he spoke excellent English – but Paula got the gist of it as Eleanor kept leaning towards her to kindly translate. The clerk, superbly cast in the moody, darkly handsome Mediterranean mould, was being polite but firm. Totally embarrassed by the fuss, Paula almost got to the stage of tugging at Eleanor's sleeve and telling her please to stop it. She was travel-weary and hot and in no mood for it. She wanted to get up to her room – it could be a broom cupboard for all she cared just now – kick off her shoes, have a shower and unpack.

However it was apparent that Eleanor was not going to be moved, not easily. All her life, Paula had worked on the principle that arguments were just not worth the pain. Luckily she and Alan were not given to arguing, not much, and when they did, it blew over quickly and was as quickly forgotten. Sometimes there were little blowouts at the card shop amongst the staff, understandably not all of them getting on, and it was Paula who generally defused the situation. Peacemaker, negotiator, smoother and soother of ruffled feathers, that was Paula. However, dealing with the juniors at work and dealing with a mad-as-hell Eleanor were not quite the same thing.

'If they think they are going to get away with this, they can think again,' Eleanor muttered. 'You have to stand firm on these things, Paula, or people will walk all over you.'

Paula sighed. For the love of heaven she couldn't see what all the fuss was about. It wasn't as if the room at the back had a view of a dustbin area because, on the contrary as the rep was quick to point out, it had a lovely view of the swimming pool at the rear and the terraced garden rising above it. In any case, they would be seeing plenty of the lake over the next two weeks and she wasn't bothered about having a balcony. As Eleanor was forking out for this, it was, however, only right and proper that she had the better room, the superior they called it.

The rep, young and harassed, looked at them, specifically at Eleanor, with a pleading look, having introduced herself on the coach as Deborah. She was made up to the nines, her make-up shiny by now, and in her uniform of patterned blouse and dark-blue winter-weight skirt, she looked as hot as Paula felt. The uniform was unflattering and made her look twice her age although perversely just now as she chewed on her lip trying to pacify the outraged Eleanor she looked like a child. Vaguely, in the delicate face, there was a look of Lucy about her, enough to cause a fluttering in Paula's heart, enough to cause her to take a deep breath which she exhaled slowly.

'It's not a problem. Really it isn't,' Paula insisted, smiling at the young girl before turning to offer Eleanor a look of reassurance.

Eleanor was flushed, her mouth tight, eyes narrowed, and somebody should tell her that being outraged was not one of her better looks. Her hair was swept up and off her face, a few stray hairs escaping now from the securing comb, and even her make-up was losing its edge. The coach trip from the airport had been horrific with the air-conditioning only partially working. Having worn the sun hat as they stood at the airport entrance waiting for the coach, Paula's short hair was flattened and, catching a glimpse of herself in the mirrored wall opposite, she tried ineffectually to fluff it up as they waited by the reception desk. Her feet, in the wedge-heeled shoes, were killing her.

Already this hotel was exceeding her wildest dreams, beating any she had experienced before because, of necessity, on the few times they had visited hotels, they had always opted for something on the cheap-and-cheerful spectrum. This one with its marble floors and extravagant displays of fresh flowers in large beautiful vases was out of this world, out of her world anyway. Although they were conducting their conversation in subdued tones a few guests, sensing trouble, glanced their way. The tour rep was now talking to the reception clerk, in English, her body language an indication of her flustered state.

'If you are quite sure you don't mind?' Eleanor said, sensing impatience and retreating a little although she ignored Paula now and looked towards Alan.

'Quite sure.' He spoke up for the first time, his voice firm.

'Leave it as it is, Eleanor. We're happy to take the room overlooking the pool. Thanks, Deborah,' he said with a smile.
'And thank you,' he added to the clerk, who gave him a nod of
appreciation.

Eleanor seemed reluctant to abandon her efforts to 'get
things sorted' but, glancing at Alan's set face and seeing she
was beaten, she gave in gracefully, accepting the rep's apology
but leaving her in no doubt that nothing else had better
go wrong or else. At her side, Paula noted that Henry had a
resigned look, noting also that he exchanged a 'you know what
women are like' look with her husband.

This was not the first irritation on the way here. There had
been a long wait at the airport at the luggage carousel – it was
lunch time – and Eleanor had nearly incited a riot there followed by an almighty fuss in the coach, where she insisted on
changing seats because the air conditioning above her first-
choice seat was working overtime with a cold draught blowing
down her neck. Paula recognized that poor Deborah would
already have marked Eleanor – and by default, the four of
them – as a potential troublemaker.

It was a relief for Paula to escape to their room for a while
having arranged to meet up later for drinks before dinner.

'Thank goodness for that,' she said, flopping down onto
the big soft bed. She loved the room and its simple but elegant
furniture – very continental – and as she lay on the bed she
could hear happy sounds from outside. People were splashing
about in the pool below, and from the pool, wide stone steps
led to a garden full of bright colours. Alan took off his shoes
and lay down beside her, reaching for her hand and giving it a
squeeze.

'Tired, sweetheart?'

She nodded but she could not idle the time away for long
because she would not rest until the unpacking was done. She
started to unpack whilst Alan had a quick shower, finding a

notice as she was doing so informing her of the small safe at the back of the cupboard for their valuables. She should be so lucky.

Eleanor, she had noticed, was wearing the Nightingale family collection: a flashy engagement ring plus another equally bonkers-sized one on her other hand, a fancy diamond-encrusted watch and a slim gold bracelet and earrings. All that, and the handbag of course, instantly recognizable as designer. The woman must have plenty because she never seemed to use the same one twice. Paula had two at any one time: a black one and a cream one which was enough to cater for any of her outfits.

Who cares? For once, she was determined not to let things like that bother her in the slightest. She was going to let things like that wash over her and just ignore it even though the little digs, more like stabbings, had been present from day one, from the very first time they met.

It was a joy to Paula that, following his spell at university, her son chose to return to Plymouth. Part of the reason was probably that he wanted to please her because after they lost Lucy she knew that Matthew was very aware that he was now the only one. Lucy's death happened when he had just started at university and he was devastated as they all were, and for a while threatened to leave and come home to be with them because he had lost interest in his course.

It meant a trip to Oxford to talk to him to persuade him otherwise. The three of them had taken a walk by the river and although she had rehearsed in her head what she would say it was Alan who took it upon himself to take his boy aside and talk privately man to man, leaving Paula to sit on a bench and watch from a distance. She was still in a state of shock, still working through the daily routine in a kind of fog, still apt to break down in tears at the oddest moments, still unable to get off to sleep because she could not get those final moments out of her head.

Sitting on the bench that day in Oxford amongst all those beautiful ancient buildings, she watched her men. Her husband and son were alike and even from a distance you could tell they were father and son. Matthew was mercifully like Alan in looks, tall and strong, and Lucy had been like her, destined to be a little lady although Lucy had more about her and would never have been afraid to speak her mind. Lucy would have never let that silly situation in the foyer today develop as it had but then Lucy would never have allowed Her Ladyship to treat her as she did. Lucy, even at thirteen, had a mind of her own.

Sitting on the bench that day in Oxford, watching her two men in the distance, the recent devastating loss still raw in her head, she had held the tears at bay as she saw them heading back.

'What did you say to him?' she asked her husband afterwards when Matthew told her he had changed his mind and would be staying to finish his course.

'Never you mind,' Alan said, taking her in his arms as he had done so often since Lucy's death. 'He's staying and he's going to do his sister proud.'

And he did.

Returning to his roots then after getting his degree, Matthew might be working for an architect's firm in the city centre but, as he was quick to point out, he would have to work hard to prove himself for the next few years. Then, he might move on, he warned his mother, so she was not to start thinking that he was going to be around here forever.

It was enough for her that he was close at hand for the time being, and she had to hide her disappointment when he announced, quite rightly according to his dad, that he would not be coming to live back home but would get a place of his own in town, a bachelor pad, he called it, which turned out to be a lot-to-be-desired bedsit over a shop in a student-digs area.

She could not pretend that she liked that idea, which seemed daft to say the least when he could stay at home for a nominal rent, but Alan persuaded her that it was better that he had his own place because he was a grown man now and not the boy they had dispatched to university. He and Lucy had been close, the five-year age gap perfect, with none of the usual brother/sister bickerings. Lucy thought the sun shone out of her big brother, Matthew was very protective of his little sister and her sudden death had knocked them back but, looking back, Matthew, aside from that immediate gut-reaction threat to leave university, had coped well with it.

At least, on the surface.

He worked hard, was liked by his superiors and clients alike, so unsurprisingly he was on the fast track now and she was so very proud of him. She kept his bedroom more or less as it had been when he was at university and home for the holidays but she did not keep it as a shrine just as Lucy's old room was not a shrine either. Her room became the study, a grand title for the small bedroom, completely redecorated with all trace of her removed.

They put the computer and a little desk in and Alan began to use it more and more as a bolt-hole. His disappearing up there in the evening did not bother her in the slightest, leaving her free to watch what she wanted on television – all the rubbish stuff – and, after a hard day standing on her feet at the shop, she was glad to slip off her shoes and put her feet up.

They had lived in this house since the children were small; tempted to move after Lucy died but, although they half-heartedly put the house on the market, it did not sell and in the end they withdrew it. Lucy was gone and would still be gone no matter where they lived and Paula liked the house and the area and had a lot of friends round here, so they decided to stay put until such time as they were coming up to retirement when they might opt for something else.

She liked making plans, although of course things did not always follow that plan: but that was called Life, wasn't it?

For a while then, for a few years following Matthew's return to Plymouth, things went reasonably well. He was still learning the ropes at work and he had a way to go before he earned enough to be comfortably off, but in the meantime he was a handsome sociable soul and there were a few girlfriends, some of whom he brought home but none of them particularly serious. There was a teenage romance just before he went off to university and that had seemed worryingly intense for a while because Chrissie was in the Lower Sixth at school coming up to seventeen: a child from a broken home with a big chip on her slender shoulders. It was obvious to Paula that the poor child was on the lookout for a substitute family because her own was so disjointed, but, although Paula tried her best, she was uneasy about it, particularly so when Chrissie seemed to be spending more time with them than with her own mother. She knew Matthew cared for the girl and had been upset when she went off with her mother and stepdad to live in Kent so suddenly that it was very nearly a moonlight flit. But the teenage relationship would not have stayed the course in any event, not when he went off to Oxford and he met up with older, more sophisticated young women.

Matthew, hurt and disappointed, imagining Chrissie to be the love of his life, had slumped into a depression for a while immediately after her departure and it was Lucy who pulled him out of it, young Lucy whom he chose to talk to, not her.

To this day, though, whenever anybody said anything about that time, when various things were recalled, Chrissie's name was noticeably absent from Matthew's reminiscences.

*

The rest of the people on the tour group seemed a nice bunch and, meeting some of them again in the hotel bar, Paula was relieved that she had chosen a suitable dress for their first evening meal because they had all scrubbed up well. She had chosen Alan's outfit for the evening, nothing new there for he had no interest whatsoever in clothes, and she was pleased that he looked as smart as any of the other men; but then in her eyes he always looked pretty good with no signs yet of losing his hair, which was still the same fairish colour, nor of gaining a paunch. He did not visit the gym nor did he exercise that much so it was more to do with luck and good genes than anything else. Her genes were not in the same category and it didn't seem quite fair for she needed to colour her hair now to cover the grey hairs and she only had to look at a cream cake to gain a few pounds.

She and Alan managed a stroll round the garden in the late-afternoon sunshine but there was no sign of Eleanor and Henry and they were glad about that. They knew it would be difficult, that they would be in each other's pockets most of the time but they did hope that they might be given a free rein at some point. There were several optional day trips on offer and they might decline some of them if they could get away with it without causing offence.

'There you are.' Eleanor powered towards them wearing a long-brightly coloured silk dress cinched at the waist with a broad belt that showed off her slim figure. She was clever with her hair and it was now curling softly around her shoulders but clipped up with a gold pin at one side. Paula was grateful that Eleanor had opted for flat sandals as, with her own high-heeled shoes, their height difference was thus minimized. 'You look lovely,' Eleanor said, smiling down at her. 'What a pretty colour. Doesn't she look lovely, Henry?'

Henry looked at her appreciatively, taking her in from top

to toe, which made her feel uncomfortable. For some reason, Henry unnerved her. There was something about him that she did not like and her womanly intuition told her to avoid being in a one-to-one situation with him. Alan thought him prickly too, but she was trying to be generous, aware that first impressions could be deceptive and that it was unwise to jump to conclusions. The longest conversation she and Henry had had together had been at the wedding reception when they sat side by side at the top table. Henry made a beautiful speech but then he had a lovely speaking voice although, sitting near to him, she was aware that he was finding it hard to contain his emotion as he spoke about his lovely daughter whom he had just given away. She liked that. It proved he was a father who cared, although judging from the brief embrace she had seen him give his daughter he may not always show his feelings.

Nicola was beautiful, with her mother's build and her father's hazel eyes, looking spectacularly beautiful on her wedding day in a simple cream dress. Thinking of what might have been if Lucy had lived had made that moment particularly hard, for she would surely have been a bridesmaid and she had fought to hold back tears knowing as she caught Alan's gaze that he was thinking precisely what she was thinking.

All these years on, Lucy still intruded into her mind and she wished she had not done so just now as the four of them stood in the bar of the hotel by the lake on the first evening of their holiday.

'You look very nice, Paula,' Henry said, prompted by his wife. 'Good choice.'

'Thank you.' Paula stopped herself in time from saying that her dress had been a bargain, reduced significantly because of a tiny flaw that nobody could see unless they were told about it. She must stop doing that, very nearly apologizing to Eleanor for every damned thing. The dress was hyacinth blue, her favourite colour, and, although her hair would never be in the same category as Eleanor's she thought the short blunt cut suited her and showed off the pretty, sparkly, dangly earrings that, aside from her wedding band, were her only jewellery.

It did not seem as if their group was going to stick together as couples quickly dispersed once in the dining room but of course the four of them were shown to a table set for four. Predictably, it was not acceptable to Eleanor being in the centre of the room but the waiter was unfazed and found them one which gave them a view of the gardens, the busy coast road and the smooth blue waters of the lake beyond.

'This reminds me of a hotel we go to a lot near St Ives,' Eleanor said once they were fussily settled, the waiter pulling out seats for the ladies and being super-attentive. 'We must take you there sometime. You'll love it. Do you get over to Cornwall much?'

'Just as far as Matthew and Nicola's but not very often to the depths,' Alan said with a smile. To Paula's relief, he seemed relaxed but then he was always much more at ease with Nicola's parents than she was. Their fancy house, the expensive clothes, the travelling, their status in the community … it did nothing for him at all. She had asked Alan how much the Nightingales were worth and he just shrugged, not the least interested. 'With me working a lot of weekends, we never seem to have the time to do the sights. I don't suppose you get over to Plymouth much?'

'No, and never for pleasure.' Eleanor gave a small shudder. 'I have to be at the gallery occasionally to check on things but I have to confess I prefer Exeter although nothing compares to Bath, which is my absolute favourite city. Have you been?'

'We honeymooned there,' Paula told her, feeling herself blush. Her fair skin easily took on colour which might have been sweet once upon a time but was embarrassing at her age. 'Alan's very interested in Roman history.'

'On his honeymoon?' Henry laughed and flashed her a look which again unsettled her before turning to his wife. 'Where the hell did we go for ours, my darling?'

'We toured France in that blue convertible of yours, as if you don't know,' she said, pausing as the waiter arrived to take their orders. Eleanor spoke to him in Italian, which pleased him although he immediately slipped into charming, heavily accented English when he realized that she was the only Italian speaker at their table.

Paula felt a little annoyed that Eleanor felt it necessary to explain the menu to her. It was in Italian of course but there was an English translation, for heaven's sake, and she wished that Eleanor would not treat her as if she was a complete idiot. She had been to Bella Italia after all, so she was not completely ignorant about pasta and what have you, although Alan was happier with English food or an occasional curry but he gamely ordered the risotto starter.

Henry took it upon himself to choose the wine – taking some considerable time over it – and she supposed she was grateful for that because she knew Alan was no wine connois-seur, although he didn't mind a drop of decent stuff. Henry's 'Would you prefer a beer, Al?' was received with a mere shake of the head and no comment. She wished Henry would not call him Al, as nobody else did. Underneath the table she felt the pressure of Alan's leg on hers, knew he was trying to reassure her that it didn't matter, that the others really were not aware that their attitude could be construed as patronizing and that it just wasn't worth worrying about.

All this was conveyed in that simple pressure of his leg and she smiled at him, at them, determined to let go and just enjoy the evening.

Chapter Five

IT WAS LATE, but still warm, on the balcony of their room and, having kicked off her shoes and dress, slipping on a silk dressing gown over her underwear, Eleanor delighted in the feel of the cool tiles against her bare feet, finally feeling relaxed after the long day. Travelling was such a bore, but a necessary evil and now they were here, on the shores of her favourite Italian lake, it was all worthwhile.

She pondered a moment, looking out across the lake as the sun lowered in the sky. There was no activity on the lake, the steamers moored for the night, and everything was very still. The remembered evening scent, the scent of Italy, drifting upwards from the garden reminded her of previous holidays spent here. She loved it all, this Veneto region, Tuscany, Rome of course, and the distinct flavour of the south coast and Capri. It had captured her heart from the very first visit and she adored the beautiful melodic tone of the language; operas were just meant to be sung in this language. Henry loved this country too but not in the romantic way she did, but then, despite the flowery compliments he was capable of from time to time, he did not possess a romantic bone in his body. She wondered if he had ever really loved her or if he had simply succumbed to what was considered a 'good' marriage and yes, that sort of thing did happen even today. She wondered why everybody drew a sharp breath when the words 'arranged marriage' were talked of, because they could be very success-ful as she and Henry had proved. At least that was the way they chose to present it to the world. In truth, she stuck with him and he with her because, as they were also business part-ners, it was a damned sight easier to do that than to go through the horrors of separation and all it would involve.

She leaned against the parapet and breathed in the evening air. Of the Italian lakes, was this her favourite? Como was much smaller, hemmed in by the mountains, but it had its own charm and Maggiore with its islands and flowers was mag-nificent but Lake Garda and its position close to Verona and Venice, again rating amongst her favourite cities in the whole world, was special.

'Good to be back, eh?' Henry appeared at her side, his hand circling her waist. He had drunk a little too much of the very good wine he had chosen, more than she had anyway, but he could hold his drink. 'I hope you aren't going to complain any more about the hotel. I like it and even you couldn't complain about the food tonight. I thought it was exceptional.'

'I don't complain for the sake of it,' she said. 'But you're right. It was a lovely meal.'

'You look beautiful tonight and you smell gorgeous,' he said, lifting her hair and nuzzling her neck. 'I could see old Al eyeing you up.'

'Don't be ridiculous. He only has eyes for Paula.'

'More fool him. You were the best-looking woman there tonight. By far.'

'Was I?' She laughed low, leaning her head against him. Compliments came easily to Henry, but they were always welcome whether or not he really meant them. 'You don't look so bad yourself for a middle-aged man.'

'Less of that. I don't feel middle-aged. To tell you the truth, sometimes these days I feel about a hundred.'

'That's work for you.' Before the nuzzling became too intense, she turned and they went back inside their room. 'You work too hard and there's really no need for you to make all those trips to London when we have people there to look after things. You should be thinking about retiring, Henry.'

'I'm only fifty-bloody-six. And what would I do if I retired? And don't say play golf because I hate it. I only do it because it's good for contacts.'

She glanced at him, knowing she had spoilt the mood, for it was true that he had no interests other than the business he had run successfully for the last twenty-five years or so. It was amazing it was going strong in these difficult financial times, but there were still an awful lot of people out there who could afford the small items of furniture and high-class collectibles that they showed and sold in their galleries dotted about the West Country. Henry imported the furniture from abroad, his contacts long established, and they could offer something different that appealed to their clients.

The Internet meant that their client base had broadened; people who returned when they were on the lookout for a difficult-to-find item. They had also attracted the eye of an excellent up-and-coming interior designer in London who now knew exactly where to come when she was on the lookout for a particular item for her clients. Eleanor considered it vulgar to name-drop, but she knew for a fact that a couple of well-known actors had a few of their collectibles in their homes courtesy of this particular lady.

'We should have a boardroom in the middle of the golf course for signing contracts,' Henry went on in a grumbling tone. 'The number of deals struck between the tenth and eleventh hole is unbelievable. Small-fry stuff admittedly but it all helps. For instance I persuaded Reggie Lord to take on that bloody awful frosted glass ashtray you found in that flea market in Caen. Who wants an ashtray these days? You can't give them away, but he was more than happy to part with three hundred and we only paid a few euros, didn't we?'

'I know it was frightful but it had the name and the seller had no idea of the significance.'

'Doesn't that make you feel guilty?'

'Why should it? I can't be held responsible if people don't do their research. I did tell you somebody would buy it. Let's not talk about work,' she said, making an effort to lighten his mood. 'Not tonight. Do you think Paula and Alan are enjoying it so far?'

'We've only just got here but I think they are, although we could have done without the hoo-hah down in reception. Did you notice Paula's face? She wanted the floor to swallow her up. My God, Eleanor, you certainly know how to create a scene.'

'It was a matter of principle.'

He huffed. 'You and your principles. Anyway, back to Al and for a man who claims to know bugger-all about wine, he certainly seemed to recognize my choice as a good one. Unless he was bluffing of course but I don't think so.' He frowned a little. 'We shouldn't underestimate him. There might be more to him than meets the eye. He's brighter than I thought.'

'I like him,' she said carefully, knowing that Henry was a jealous man and might misinterpret the remark. 'For somebody like him, he's very nice.'

'Somebody like him?' Henry laughed. 'That is one of the reasons I was against this trip. We have nothing in common with the Walkers. Matthew might well be their son, but he has grown away from them and it happened the day he went off to Oxford. It's a bit sad but there you are. If I didn't know him better I could say that he's now a touch ashamed of them, particularly his mother. She doesn't seem to know much about anything, does she? There's not a lot between those little ears.'

'Matthew adores his mother, darling. I think that's quite a mean thing for you to say. Don't you remember he told us right away what his father did? He's not ashamed of it in the least.'

'Isn't he? A bloody driving instructor?'

'At least he runs his own business.'

'If you can call it that. He's been near to packing it in a couple of times, he told me. He struggles to make a decent living.'

'Oh. I thought he was doing rather well.' She gave him a look. 'So, you two do talk, then?'

'We have to talk about something and it's usually work-based, although I'm not sure he understands much about the art world. Mind you, it's no picnic what he does. He has nerves of steel. You should hear some of the stories he tells. Thank God for a dual-control car, he says.' Henry laughed, leaning to switch on the bedside lamps before starting to undress. 'I'm having a bath. It's big enough, care to join me?'

'I'm exhausted. I'll have a shower in the morning. You can wake me up early if you like?' she said, tossing him the invitation but making it clear, she hoped, that tonight she just wanted to slip between those covers and go to sleep.

The air conditioning buzzed gently all night long and, in the middle of the night, Eleanor got up and turned it off. Then, taking care not to wake a snoring Henry, she opened the window, much preferring the night noises that crossed the lake.

They were an hour adrift, time-wise, but she rather hoped that Henry would sleep through so that any thoughts of love-making at dawn would have to wait.

Chapter Six

THE HOTEL WHERE she worked was across the border in Devon, several miles down a country lane bounded with high-bank hedges. The short drive normally soothed Nicola, whatever the weather, whatever the season, but today, rattled by the argument with her husband last night, she was still feeling stressed as she approached.

The gardens at Nethersley Hall were in full glorious bloom at this time of year as she drove down the narrow approach drive, past the sunken garden with its charming water feature, parking her car in the staff car park that was sited unobtrusively off to one side. The house was a Jacobean manor, originally a family home, the long gallery supposedly haunted. She was far too pragmatic to believe that, but she had to admit that last year on one of those dark December days, she was alone in the long gallery and as she reached the end of it she felt a distinct chill and heard a rustle of silk close by.

Each bedroom had its unique character, with rich old wood panelling and beautiful pieces of antique furniture, exquisite plasterwork, not to mention the most gorgeous window dressings. The ultimate in honeymoon delight was the honeymoon suite, with its four-poster bed and, following their wedding, the bride and groom often chose to spend their first night together there. Sitting together in front of a log fire, the heavy curtains drawn across, enjoying a glass of wine and a light supper, it was indeed a perfect way to start off a marriage.

She spotted one of the gardeners – the chatty one with the beard – at work in one of the borders but, even though she saw out of the corner of her eye that he had put down whatever implement he was using in preparation for one of his inter-minable and incredibly boring chats, she deliberately avoided direct eye contact because he only had one topic of conversation and whether or not the rabbits had been causing havoc again was no concern of hers. She did, however, have the grace to acknowledge his presence with a wave of her hand as she hurried by.

As she neared the entrance, a heaven of scented wisteria surrounding the impressive porch, she spotted a couple of the junior staff slouching outside, leaning against the wall in full view of everyone, smoking and laughing. They glanced at her, totally unconcerned, and she felt a flash of annoyance, in no mood this morning for any further hassle. She may not be that much older than they but she was a hell of a lot more senior and she was not going to let the insolence pass her by. Once you did that, they had you down as a soft touch.

'What on earth do you think you are doing?' she said, homing in on them.

They stared at her, speechless for a moment, although the girl's eyes narrowed and her mouth pursed. She was one of the housekeeping staff with over-made-up eyes and a lot of fluffy blonde hair. A nose-stud too. Good God, what were they thinking of, employing somebody with a nose-stud?

'What does it look like?' the girl said, taking another drag, gangster-like, on her cigarette as a couple of guests came by. By moving slightly and offering the guests a broad smile and a 'Good morning' Nicola hoped they would not notice the others.

'If you must smoke there is a designated area at the rear,' she went on, her smile vanishing as she confronted the youngsters once more.

'Yes, miss.' The young man – one of the waiting staff – grinned, not taking her remotely seriously.

'It's Mrs Walker to you and if I catch either of you here again, I shall report you to Mr Gilbert.' She waited a moment for that to sink in, looking at their name-tags and making sure they noticed that. 'Now, go somewhere else. And tie up your hair, Tiffany,' she added to the girl. 'It's most unhygienic wearing it loose.'

The girl held her ground but her cheeks flushed and she was the first to look away. Tugging at the boy's sleeve she gave the signal for them to disappear and, with a final withering glance from the young man, they scooted off. Nicola caught the word 'cow' but it hardly mattered. She was not here to be popular. One day she would be events manager and after that, who knows what she might achieve? She had dreams of starting up on her own, something to do with events planning but she was not ready yet for that. One thing was sure, the job here was just a stepping stone and she did not see herself here in the long term.

Glancing at her watch, she guessed that the parents would be up in the air by now and she hoped to goodness they had a good holiday together. Nicola knew her mother far too well and she did not trust her motives for inviting the Walkers on this holiday. Whatever her mother got up to, there was always something behind it. Her mother, like it or not, did tend to lord it over everybody and that was fine as long as people respected that. But she knew that Eleanor was not liked in all quarters, that she was considered to be overbearing and too outspoken for some and she just hoped that she was doing this, being charitable, for the right reasons and not because, in some devious way, she was trying to undermine Paula.

Wearing a bright-blue fascinator atop her blonde hair at the wedding, Paula had looked very nice, her mother said, although she did add that it must be so difficult for somebody as tiny as that to find anything to fit properly. The Walker side of the family, determined not to let the side down, had done Matthew proud, the ladies mostly wearing over-the-top hats and a selection of frilly and floral frocks, seemingly unfazed by the Nightingale contingent whose hats were a little more restrained, their dresses elegant in their simplicity although there was a fair sprinkling of outrageous Jimmy Choos. Her funny cousin Philly was wearing a strapless frock that showed off the tattoo that snaked down her arm. Oddly enough it had been Philly who had happily, glass of champagne in hand, surged towards the Walker side of the room at the reception, her raucous laugh livening up proceedings.

'Really ...' She remembered her mother's dismay. 'I can't think what your aunt Andrea is thinking of. In the old days, Philly would have been tucked away and not allowed within sight of anybody of any significance. As for the tattoo, well, words fail me.'

Nicola agreed the tattoo was a bit off, but she half regretted the easy way Philly got on with everybody, leaving everybody smiling, Matthew included. Surely every family is allowed one black sheep.

Matthew won those snooty Nightingale ladies over, his speech both funny and sincere. He was in a profession they thoroughly approved of and had been to Oxford at that, the proper university that is, so his former attendance at a comprehensive, an inner-city one, could be glossed over. Snobbery among the Nightingale clan was still a force to be reckoned with, proud as they were of a thin trace of blue blood in their ancestry, but she and Matthew were able to laugh it off, although she knew that Paula was painfully aware of it too and could not shake it off quite as easily.

She still recalled that first meeting at home where Paula had seemed overwhelmed by the house and grounds, as well she might be, saying to Matthew later that there was no way she could ever invite them to their home. Her mother had played the part of gracious hostess to a tee, alarmingly regal with the best china on show, the delicate cup looking quite ridiculous in Alan's hands.

'We normally use mugs,' her father had said with a grin, trying to put them at ease but rewarded for that remark with a glare from her mother.

After the wedding, Nicola hoped that the two families would continue to see each other from time to time, but there was no need for intimacy and this holiday together worried her a lot. Being in close proximity for two whole weeks did seem to be a recipe for disaster and she just knew that, sooner or later, somebody would blow a fuse.

Her father-in-law Alan was a lovely quiet man but he was very protective of his wife. It was nauseatingly sweet in fact that the two of them were obviously so devoted to each other. If Paula was threatened or upset in any way, Alan would speak his mind because his little wife could not possibly defend herself. He could see right through Eleanor, Nicola could see that, and she wondered if her mother was aware of that. She had seen the surprise in her mother's eyes when she first met Alan. He was so unlike Matthew, whose fetching personality made him both likeable and charming, the rougher edges of his West Country accent worn away by the years at university. Alan was a man of the old school, suspicious of strangers and particularly suspicious of strangers with money, and you could almost see the brain ticking away under the calm exterior. He was every bit as handsome as Matthew, though, with warm brown eyes, a man of few words compared with her mother's monumental vocabulary. She supposed that his caring manner, akin to a sympathetic bedside one, would be ideal for soothing the nerves of the learner drivers he sat beside day after day.

As for Paula, predictably she worked as an assistant in a shop in town selling greetings cards and the like; a shop which Eleanor now avoided on her visits to Plymouth because it was just too embarrassing to see Paula in there wearing her uniform. Eleanor was retired from her teaching post having given it up years ago to help her father with the business, her linguistic skills proving very useful in his dealings with his European contacts. Her mother's flair for languages was to be admired, but Nicola hoped she would not try to converse with the locals as that would look like she was showing off in Matthew's mother's eyes. Paula had the biggest inferiority complex she had ever come across.

Awkward was the only word she could think of to describe the whole set-up.

The four of them had nothing in common. On the one hand, a driving instructor and a shop assistant; on the other, an entrepreneur specializing in fine arts and his lady wife, a former teacher and linguist, who liked to think she was a touch above.

It would only end in tears.

'Hello, Barbara. How are you?' Nicola said, heels clicking as she tapped her way into the hotel and the polished dark oak of the reception desk. It promised to be another fine warm day and already she was feeling over dressed in the suit, tights on at that, but it was important to look the part and Gerry Gilbert, the manager, was very keen that the dress code amongst the staff, senior or otherwise, was observed.

'I'm good, thanks.' Barbara nodded, giving her a quick once-over, glance hovering a moment at her stomach. Barbara had caught her being sick in the ladies' loo a week ago and was now convinced she was pregnant, which was not true. Absolutely not true. 'No major problems to speak of. We've got the terrace tables ready for lunch and we are fully booked but you may have noticed that it's getting a bit breezy so we may have to abandon them.'

'Have you checked the forecast?'

'Not yet.' Barbara had been here forever and she thought she ran the place but Nicola had already discovered a few loopholes in her efficiency. The woman was stuck in her ways and she needed to up her game.

'Then wouldn't it be a good idea to do that?'

'I was going to,' Barbara said, not giving an inch. 'But you know what it's like here. In this valley we're in a kind of climate cocoon. Weather passes us by. I've found the best thing is to ignore the forecast and just to look out of the window.'

Nicola had no time for further discussion about the weather and with a final brief smile breezed on.

They were full, more or less, which was good news but good weather now and for the next month would mean repeat bookings, so Nicola looked anxiously out of the window as she went through the 'quiet' adult-only lounge on her way to the meeting with Gerry, passing through the long gallery where a couple of guests were taking morning coffee. She acknowledged them with a breezy smile, pausing to pass the time of day before continuing.

There was a wedding coming up in a few weeks, preparations in full swing, as well as a small corporate event in a few days' time in the form of drinks and nibbles, which Emma had handed over to her as her first solo venture. It was something of a coup because Emma was notoriously uneasy about delegating. Emma, who was in overall charge of the events team, was very efficient, calm, confident and controlled and a wonderful mentor and Nicola hoped that, by the time Emma moved on – a move back up to her beloved north with her partner was long threatened – she would be deemed ready to step into the lady's shoes.

She made sure she was well thought of by Emma and Gerry, adopting an agreeable stance with them, so that when the time came for Emma to go, her enthusiasm and gathering expertise would not pass unnoticed. If, on the other hand, Emma's move up north proved to be just wishful thinking on her part, then she would herself move onwards and upwards, where to she had no idea but it certainly would not be the north. Matthew could do his job from anywhere so there wouldn't be a problem in persuading him to move. She liked this area well enough but there were some equally attractive areas spread around and staying put seemed rather a dull option.

She thought briefly of her parents, well on the way to Italy by now, and of Matthew's too. The Walkers had flown before but not very often and she knew that Paula was nervous, but they were on a tour and it was a one-class-only affair on the chartered flight, which would mean her mother having to rough it this time.

Although her mother normally abhorred these sorts of tours on 'Riff-Raff Air', this particular tour was of the top-notch variety as her mother had been at pains to point out, certainly not one of these cheapo affairs based at a budget hotel, and they were staying at a high-class hotel in a prime location on the shores of the Italian lake. Interested in hotels from a professional viewpoint, Nicola had looked it up and it certainly looked most impressive, very nearly as impressive as this one.

She entered the manager's office, where Emma was already there beside Gerry Gilbert, smiling broadly at them and offering them a cheerful good morning, before closing the door. She did not give a hoot about offending the junior staff but when it came to the big knobs it made sense to keep on the right side of them.

The parents, all four of them, would be absolutely fine, she told herself as she eased herself into a chair, and if not, then there was nothing she could do about it.

*

Nicola and Matthew shared a smile and a kiss when they got back and it seemed that both of them had decided on their way home to forget the earlier heated exchange, so it was not mentioned other than a muttered 'Sorry' as they kissed.

'I hope they got there all right,' Nicola said as they sat down at the kitchen table to eat. 'Mum has turned off her mobile and says that I must not, under any circumstances, try to contact her unless it's an emergency.'

'My mother probably forgot to take hers along,' Matthew said with a smile. 'She hates the thing. Dad did say much the same thing, though, about getting in contact. Give us a break, he said, and leave us in peace.'

'So that's what we will do.' Nicola spread a chunky roll with the butter substitute. They only had wine at the weekend and, contrary to her expectations about this evening, Matthew had not relaxed the rule so it was just water and she took a sip, relaxing at last after a busy day. They tried not to talk shop if possible but what else was there to talk about? The subject of Paula was to be avoided at all costs. 'That wedding I was telling you about is cancelled,' she said. 'We only heard today and they've asked for a refund on their deposit so although we are not strictly obliged, we'll probably sort something out as a gesture of goodwill.'

'Bit short notice, that. What happened?'

'How should I know? Presumably one or other of them had second thoughts. Can you believe it? How can you let it get as close as that and then abandon it? They seemed such a nice couple too when I showed them round. They held hands the whole time.' She chewed on her bread thoughtfully. 'Although now I come to think of it, they were a bit too lovey-dovey if you get my meaning? And I did see him looking at Pamela … you know her, the brunette in reception?'

'Right. She is quite eye-catching,' he said, smiling hugely.

'And she flirts.'

'Does she? Oh. Don't tell me she tried flirting with you?'

'She certainly did. That afternoon when I came to pick you up … you remember when your car was in the garage … she couldn't have made it clearer that she fancied me if she had been doing a pole dance half-naked.'

'You are joking?' she said, watching his face, uncertain because sometimes he was hard to read. 'I think you flatter yourself, Mr Walker, if you think she was interested in you. She has a very hot boyfriend.'

'So?' He shrugged and they laughed.

Nicola liked the banter, also quite liked the fact that other women fancied her husband, as well they might. Later, as Matthew went into the little study to finish off some paperwork, she read a few more pages of her paperback although she was finding it hard to concentrate. The cancellation of the wedding had thrown her a little, jolted her, made her realize that sometimes things did go wrong. Poor girl if she had been jilted: the dress bought, the bridesmaids chomping at the bit, all the guests having to be put off at the very last minute, gifts returned. What a nightmare! Poor bloke if he was the one who had been cast aside. What a blow to his pride. She tried to imagine how she would feel if it had happened to her, but of course it had not. Matthew had been there, in that pretty little church, waiting for her as she walked down the aisle on her father's arm.

She would never forget the way Matthew turned to look at her, the love in his eyes. It was true. You carried moments like that with you to your grave. Bar the odd argument and surely all couples had them, she reckoned that she was lucky to have him.

She had no fears about Matthew because he loved her and she knew she could trust him. She knew her own dad had had a few flings over the years, things she was not supposed to know about, and she knew that her mother soldiered on regardless presumably because she loved him but maybe because she could not bear for the world to know.

It would never happen with Matthew.

Like his father Alan, Matthew was a one-woman man.

Chapter Seven

'I DO KNOW THE significance of Juliet's balcony,' Paula said, irritated as Eleanor started to explain it to her as if she was a child. Once a teacher always a damned teacher. 'It's from *Romeo and Juliet* and I can even remember what Romeo said.'

Eleanor was sticking to her like glue and she so wanted to shake her off this morning. A coach had deposited them here and they could have opted, like everybody else, for a proper conducted tour of Verona with a guide, but instead Eleanor had insisted that the four of them go it alone. After all, hadn't she been before, three times, so she knew all there was to know about the place and she found it all a little frustrating being shepherded around in a gang as if they were tourists.

Wasn't that exactly what they were?

'Oh. You've heard of *Romeo and Juliet*?' Eleanor seemed surprised that she should have any knowledge at all of Shakespeare but Paula remembered doing the play at school. She was a shy student, but good at remembering lines so she had been persuaded into a biggish role which, funnily enough, she rather enjoyed. She remembered still, with a delicious pride, the way the teacher had taken her aside and whispered that she had acted Shirley Walsh who was playing Juliet off the stage and asked if she was considering a career in acting. It was stupid to even think of that, although in fact she recalled how good it felt to be up there on stage pretending to be somebody else.

Her mother was surprised when her English teacher had repeated the words at the following open evening but, although she had not said anything to the teacher, she had not offered much in the way of encouragement on the way home. A single mother, she had worked her fingers to the bone to do the best for her daughter – as she was so fond of saying – but she had no ambition other than to keep their heads above water and to be able to afford little treats from time to time. She couldn't wait for Paula to leave school and get a job.

'That teacher doesn't know what she's talking about. Who do we know who's gone to acting school? She's no right to be putting daft ideas in your head,' was the best she could manage when Paula dared to mention the acting. Of course it was just a dream and remained a dream. Once, though, she read an article about a famous actress who revealed that she was pitifully shy in real life but threw off her shyness as soon as she stepped onto the stage into whatever role she might be playing.

If only she could do that too, because sometimes she was frustrated by the shyness that still overtook her – usually at the wrong moment. For instance, she wanted desperately to say to Eleanor, 'Shut up, you old bat, and stop patronizing me,' but of course she never would, not in a million years. As for knowing about *Romeo and Juliet*, she thought she might still be able to recite the entire part of Juliet's nurse given the appropriate cue. So, how dare Eleanor make the assumption that she had never heard of the play?

'Sorry.' Eleanor smiled, blissfully unaware of how much she was offended. 'I thought you might not know much about Shakespeare.'

'Well, I do.' Paula sighed, waving her information sheet with the little map of Verona in front of her face like a fan. Having lost the men, the two of them had been wandering around the labyrinth of old streets for ever and it was so hot and she felt a bit sick as the strong scent of the sun cream drifted up to her nose. It was good of course that it was sunny, and she knew she ought not to complain, heaven forbid, but it was too hot in the middle of the day to be traipsing around the streets and what she needed now was a cooling drink. She had discarded her hat because it was making her hair feel too sticky against her neck, but there was no shade just here and she could feel the powerful heat of the sun. She should watch it or her brain might get frazzled and she needed to keep it sharp when she was dealing with Eleanor.

'I love it here,' Eleanor said. 'I love the people. Have you noticed how they parade about in the evening wearing their best clothes and strutting their stuff?'

'They look very smart,' Paula admitted, thinking that the poor youngsters at home could not compete with the easy style of the young people here.

'It's called *la passeggiata*, a sort of showing-off to each other. At least it's better than throwing up in the gutter, which our youngsters seem to do at home. It's got worse or are we getting old, Paula? I never got drunk when I was young, not deliberately. Did you?'

'No I didn't. I don't much like drinking although we've had some lovely wine here.'

'All Italian, you notice. They don't do French or Australian wines. I love that.' Eleanor laughed. 'Do you fancy a drink? Non-alcoholic of course.'

'I'd love one and a sit-down for a while. My feet are killing me. Where have the men got to?'

'I have no idea.' Eleanor glanced around and then shrugged. 'It doesn't matter. They know where to pick up the coach. Let's get ourselves a lemonade. Come on.'

She set off, a vision in a flowing ankle-length white cotton dress, a silky pink scarf casually draped around her neck, various items of silver jewellery hanging from her ears and around her wrist. Unlike Paula, she was wearing flats, a much more sensible choice for a walking tour. Her hair was in a pigtail today, a statement style, a heavy solitary twist secured with a pink ribbon. Only somebody with as much confidence as Eleanor could get away, at her age, with a style like that. Catching a glimpse of the two of them in a shop window, Paula thought her own ensemble had pretty much hit the mark too, although she wished now that she had opted for more comfortable shoes. Trying to up her height so that she was closer to eye level with Eleanor was proving a challenge.

They found a café with outside seating and Eleanor ordered them soft drinks from the waiter – in Italian – and they settled themselves under the shade of the parasol and watched the world go by. Various languages jostled for attention; Italian, the harsher Germanic sounds, the American drawl, even some English voices – complaining, unfortunately – drifted their way.

'I adore Verona,' Eleanor said. 'Keep it to yourself, but they say that Shakespeare never visited, in fact. But you have to admit that the balcony is something special even if it's all in our imagination that it was the actual balcony.'

Paula looked at her, puzzled. It was all pure fiction.

'I hope I haven't spoilt it for you. You did know that balcony we've just seen was built sometime in the thirties?'

Paula didn't know that, but who cares? She had just watched two actors re-enacting the little scene at the balcony and it was magical. Completely oblivious, looking gorgeous as in the way of the Italian youth, several pairs of young lovers had clustered all around them, arms entwined, gazing at each other; and it reminded Paula of her youth, bringing with it of course that sadness for times long gone.

As if they were thinking the same thing, they both sighed deeply.

'This is lovely, thank you,' Paula said, suddenly aware that she had never thanked her properly for all this. They had offered to pay something but Eleanor had seemed affronted at the very idea of that, although Alan took some persuading because he did not want to be in her debt.

They might not be in the same league as Henry and Eleanor's business, but Alan was doing OK because people still needed to learn to drive whatever the economic climate. He had a good reputation as an instructor but the prices had been pegged for a while now and they were feeling the pinch. They were cautious with money and although she often accused Alan of being tight, she was also built in that mould and did not like to spend their hard-earned money foolishly. They had a nice amount saved and she took pleasure in adding a little to it each month, although what the hell they were saving up for she had no idea because there was only Matthew to leave it to and he was in a good job earning a good salary so he did not need it. Still, she liked to dwell occasionally on the savings which she knew would see them through not only a rainy day, but a monsoon. 'We appreciate it, Eleanor,' she added, determined, though, that they would reciprocate in some way at a later date. The last thing she wanted was for Nicola's mother to think they were spongers. 'It is very kind of you.'

'Not at all. Henry's rolling in it. I help out but he does the bulk of the work, the boring nitty-gritty stuff. I asked you to come because we need some time together to get to know each other. After all, one day we will share a grandchild, won't we? I can hardly wait, although if I know my daughter it's not going to happen for a while yet.'

Paula nodded, half-listening to the chat from the nearby table. It was pleasant in the shade under the parasol and the little blocks of ice jostled against each other in her glass as she sipped the cool liquid. Eleanor had ordered ice-cream as well, which she was quickly realizing was nothing like the ice-cream back home. Italian ice-cream was something else. 'I don't think Matthew's in a hurry to have children either,' she said. 'Not that he's said anything but it's just the impression I get.'

'No, we must be patient,' Eleanor agreed. 'They don't seem in a rush to have children these days. Nicola is doing very well at the hotel and I know she wants to build a career in hospitality management, there or somewhere else. They won't move far, though, I can assure you of that. She loves this area.'

'Matthew did say he might move once upon a time, but now that he's married I think he will think twice about it. When two of you have got to find new jobs it isn't as easy, is it?'

'Absolutely not. Fortunately we have never had that problem. I thoroughly enjoyed teaching but when Henry's business expanded into Europe, my knowledge of languages was really helpful, so I started to go with him on his trips and I decided at that point to give up the teaching.' She smiled a little. 'It was becoming a little too stressful, Paula. I was teaching older children and these days some of them are seventeen going on thirty-five and they think they know it all already.'

'Matthew says you travel to France a lot.'

'Yes, we do. We pick up wonderful stuff from the open markets and house sales in France, sometimes things with a client specifically in mind. We get things for a bargain price and then sell them on. One person's tat is precious to another person and it's just a question of matching up items with the right people. The French have always been so stylish and their furniture has that edge. It's very exciting.'

'It sounds it.' Paula smiled, wondering if Eleanor expected her to try to compete with that. As if she could, for how on earth could her job working in a card shop compete, and although people thought Alan's job was a doddle, it most certainly was not. You had to have patience, a lot of it, to cope with what he had to put up with. Some of these would-be drivers had a death wish from the word go and one dear lady, a long-time pupil, insisted on continuing with her weekly lessons when the chances of her ever acquiring a licence were nil. After more than a hundred lessons, Alan had broken the news to her, being very straight with her and more or less saying he didn't want to take her money and give her false hope but she rejected that, saying it was her money and she could do what she wanted with it.

It did cross Paula's mind that the lady was madly in love with him and cherished the moments she spent with him, so perhaps she was deliberately fluffing the driving so that she could continue to see him on a weekly basis. She had told Alan and he laughed and said what on earth would she see in him? That's what she loved most about her husband. He had no idea how attractive he was to the ladies. She had seen the look Eleanor shot his way and it amused her and did not worry her for she could never imagine Her Ladyship settling for a man like Alan in a million years. Unless of course she fancied what might be thought of in her circles as 'a bit of rough'.

She would be wrong about that. Alan was a lot of things but he was not that. He was a diamond in the dust, a very intelligent man but he had never gained his full potential, giving up the chance of university to go straight into work. He did not start off as a driving instructor but he had never been out of work since leaving school and, thirsty for knowledge, had gained a degree from the Open University a few years ago, although he preferred not to tell people about that.

Paula excused herself from the outside table of the café in Verona and with some trepidation went to the Ladies. You never knew in these places whether it was going to be ultra-smart and fully tiled with mystifying fancy taps or one of the old-fashioned hole-in-the-floor affairs which she would never in a million years get used to. Thank God, it was the former and she brushed her hair and redid her lipstick before returning to the table where Eleanor was settling the bill, finishing off her conversation with the waiter and leaving what must be a lavish tip because the chap was all smiles as they left.

Next day, Paula was sunning herself at the poolside when Eleanor appeared. She hid a sigh because, although the trip out to Verona had been great, it had not been a total success because she could not escape Eleanor's clutches. They had not caught up with the men until they picked up the coach but it seemed the two gents had enjoyed themselves finding a nice restaurant to have lunch before picking up some English newspapers – yesterday's – and relaxing in a shady spot by the Arena.

Today was a free day with no planned excursions and it was something of a relief.

'I thought you would be here,' Eleanor said, arranging herself on the sun bed beside her. 'Henry's taken the boat across to Sirmione but I've seen it before and I wanted a breather. Where's Alan?'

'He's taken a stroll into town to see if he can find a museum or something,' Paula said, looking at Eleanor but keeping her sunglasses on so that she could avoid direct eye contact. She noticed, could not fail to notice, the smooth, golden-tanned legs nor the elegance of Eleanor's swimwear; a flowing beach cover-up with just a tantalizing glimpse beneath of a white bikini. She was wearing a swimsuit herself, a structured black one-piece from M&S, her bikini days long gone. 'I'm just enjoying the sunshine,' she added unnecessarily. 'Isn't it gorgeous?'

'It certainly is. If only we had weather like this in Cornwall, although when it is like this, it is absolutely beautiful on the coast. May I join you?'

Paula nodded, feeling a confession coming on. She had felt

for some days that Eleanor wanted to talk to her about something but could not quite bring herself to do it.

'You needn't answer this if you don't want to ...'

Ah.

'But Matthew did mention something about his sister and I wondered if you might like to tell me about it. I have some experience in counselling and I'm told I am a good listener,' she added with a little laugh.

There was a short silence as time stilled. Suddenly it was as if the two of them were inside a bubble with outside sounds diminished. Paula watched guests swimming and playing around in the cool blue waters of the pool, the Italian guests parading round as only they could do, but in a heartbeat she was back to that awful day, that awful October day when, to put no finer point on it, her whole world fell apart. In the blink of an eye, her life changed. They gave it a name which made it real but it didn't matter what they called it, it could have been bubonic plague for all she cared for it had the same effect.

'I'm sorry.' She roused herself with an effort, the shouts and splashes poking through her bubble and bursting it abruptly. 'If you don't mind, I really don't want to talk about it just now.'

'Of course. I'm sorry to have brought it up,' Eleanor said stiffly. 'But it really does no good to bottle things up. It's just that sometimes it helps to talk about things to a friend.'

A friend?

Were they friends? Their relationship was complicated and only brought about because they had become related – sort of – and the truth was that they would never have come across each other if Matthew had not married Nicola. Paula was still uncertain about how she felt about Nicola, the girl whom Matthew loved. She was not at ease yet with her daughter-in-law and she knew the feeling was reciprocated. It was taking time and she had not yet given up hope that they might eventually become friends.

What would Lucy make of her? Lucy, despite her young age, had been great at seeing through people and Paula had placed a lot of faith in what her daughter thought. Paula had not liked Chrissie much but then nor had she.

'What does Matty see in her?' Lucy had asked, her teenage wisdom shining through and saying what Paula had long been thinking. 'She's so needy. Clinging onto him like she does. She's like a barnacle on a boat.'

'Don't you dare say anything!'

'As if I would. Honestly, Mum, you treat me like a *child*.'

She wished Lucy was here now and she could ask her if she liked Nicola. 'What's her mum like?' Lucy would have asked.

One word sprang to mind. Shallow.

And there it was. Like mother, like daughter. Already Nicola was showing a few worrying tendencies to think and act like her mother.

God help Matthew.

Chapter Eight

IT WAS SOME time after they met before Matthew introduced Nicola to his parents. It had been a few months since that evening at the hotel and it was all ticking along nicely. There had been some dinners together, the theatre, a few trips out and although they kissed after the first date, she wanted to wait a while before going the whole hog with him. So, she kept him at arm's length until neither of them could stand it any longer, but his flat was little more than a hovel – albeit neat and tidy – and at that time she was back to living at home so meeting there was out of the question.

It felt furtive and ultimately unsatisfactory.

After graduating from university with a job in the hotel industry already lined up, Nicola got a flat-share in Barnstaple with a girlfriend but although it worked for a few years, it had to come to an end eventually and did so when the girlfriend found a man and moved out. She could not afford the place on her own and did not want to go through the hassle of trying to find some other girl to share with. Although there was the option of staff accommodation at the hotel, it was just one poky little room up in the eaves – the servants' quarters, no less and a bit reminiscent of student digs – so although moving back home was a dreadful thing to do, it did make sense.

Financially she could save some money and she had several rooms at home to call her own, and in addition, her laundry was done and her meals were cooked for her.

With several years experience under her belt, she moved jobs at that point to her current hotel, which was so very different from the modern 'safe but dull' one she had worked at before. Nethersley Hall tucked away in its secret valley – or so the brochure claimed – was a one-off, old and grand retaining much of its original style, although not at the expense of up-to-the-minute bathrooms with decent showers and so on. There were spectacular views of the Devon countryside from all the guest windows and with its antique furniture and surplus of chintz, it had a comfortable old-fashioned feel. The chef was trained in London and Paris so the cream teas they served took on a special quality.

It was not a job to be missed, a heaven-sent opportunity but it made for a longish commute from her parents' home in Cornwall. However, as she loved to drive her brand new little car – a twenty-fifth birthday present from her father – it was not a huge problem. Her mother was thrilled to have her home, her father less so, but she knew in her heart that even though she had her own space at home, things had changed. She had grown up and she objected to her mother treating her as if she was the teenager she had been before she went off to university, complaining about the state of her room, would you believe?

After a few months of sleeping together whenever they could, she and Matthew had already talked about getting somewhere together, renting a bigger place, but it was a big commitment moving in with a man and she was less sure than he was about the wisdom of it. She needed a ring on her finger first so for the moment she was holding back, but when Matthew said he wanted to introduce her to his parents she knew then that this was getting serious. And when the

PATRICIA FAWCETT

M-word was finally mentioned, it came as a surprise but a pleasant one for after all they were both well established in their careers and approaching thirty seemed as good an age as any to consider marriage.

Although Matthew had told her about his parents, not holding back from saying what they did, which immediately put them in a particular financial bracket in her head, the terraced house in the street in Plymouth had been a bit of a shock.

The area was close to the city, walking distance, and not the best district, although she liked the pastel colours of the little houses and the fact that the sea and the sound of seagulls were just around the corner. She could cope with it for she did not think of herself as a snob. She had been privately educated and counted a lot of snobs amongst her schoolfriends but she was certainly not one of them. At university she had mingled with all sorts of people, some of them from northern comprehensives, although in the end when it became obvious that attitudes you were born with were bloody hard to shift, she had drifted towards people from similar backgrounds because it was easier.

When Matthew said the name of the street where his parents lived, and not knowing the city that well, she had pictured a row of newish semi-detached properties with little front gardens and wrought-iron gates. So, seeing the little steep cobbled street with the houses directly off for the very first time, the row of ugly brown bins standing all the way along the street because it was bin day, she just about stopped herself from making a negative comment.

Matthew had driven her round and they sat outside the house a moment holding hands.

'I'm feeling a bit nervous,' she told him. 'And I can't think why. I was introduced to the Queen at university and I didn't feel nervous then.'

80

'Were you? You never said. Why was that?'

'She opened a new wing and a couple of the students were chosen to be presented and I was one of them. I had to learn to curtsey.' She smiled. 'She was lovely. A tiny lady in pink. Totally in pink. She has the loveliest smile.'

'Oh. That's something to talk about with Mum. She'll be very impressed. They are looking forward to meeting you,' he said.

'Are they? Christ, I wish I could say the same.'

'Don't say Christ when you're with them. It's not that they're religious or anything but Dad doesn't swear and I've never heard Mum say anything stronger than damn.'

She laughed. 'Bloody hell, Matthew, you mean I can't say fuck in front of them.'

He laughed too. 'No way. Mum would faint on the spot.'

'I shall be on my best behaviour, then.'

'Promise?'

She dropped the comedy. 'Yes, I promise. I wouldn't dream of embarrassing you, babe. I shall be Little Miss Goody-Two-Shoes.'

'Thanks. Now, let's fill you in. Mum will bring out the nibbles and offer you a glass of wine which she will have bought specially for you. And she will have been cleaning the house from top to bottom all day long.'

'Oh no, I hope not. I can't bear fuss.'

'She'll like you,' he said, squeezing her hand. 'Are you ready? Come on, let's get it over with.'

At the time she had not taken Matthew to her home, to meet her parents, because she knew the fuss her mother would make and she did not want to subject him to that, not yet, not when they had not long met. Although she had strong feelings already for him, although she had accepted his proposal – sort of – she was not absolutely one hundred per cent sure that it was a goer, that this was finally it. She did not know Matthew that well so it was all to do with shallow stuff, like his being so handsome that other women looked at him in *that* way when she was with him and it made her feel marvellous.

'He's mine, all mine,' she wanted to say. 'So back off.'

She was hesitating while there was still time to back out without it being a major deal. It was all very well for her mother to talk, but things were different then, more black and white, and nowadays the colours were smudged and, perhaps because they jumped into bed more quickly than maybe her mother and certainly her grandmother's generation did, then moving on to the next step – that awful word 'commitment' – was harder than ever.

'Pleased to meet you, Nicola,' Paula Walker said at their first meeting in the narrow hall of the house. She had obviously had her hair done that day, for it looked incredibly stiff in its short style. She held out her hand and Nicola grasped it, surprised at how little she was, even smaller than the Queen, taking in at a glance the effort the woman had gone to, on a limited budget obviously, to make the little house homely. There was an aroma of baking bread and coffee as if she had the house up for sale and Nicola was a potential buyer.

'Hello Paula. It's nice to meet you too.'

She thrust the flowers at her, several bunches of daffodils because it was spring, and Paula blushed and told her she shouldn't have, before scurrying off to find a vase, leaving Nicola to meet Matthew's dad, who had come out of the room they called the lounge to greet her. Shaking his hand, a warm full grip, she saw straight off something of Matthew in the older man. The same easy demeanour, he being not the least concerned that she was perhaps a little different from the other girls Matthew might have brought home; whereas Paula's anxious fluttering and wide-eyed awe as if she was of royal blood was an irritation that was instant and would prove to be constant.

The second time she visited Matthew's parents, a few months on with the relationship now firmly established and a diamond ring on her finger, Paula did not disappoint and produced the family photograph albums, proudly showing her pictures of Matthew when he was little; an energetic bright-looking child with that same unruly hair and wide smile. As Paula turned the pages, Matthew grew older, school photos galore and then there he was, much more recognizable as a teenager, with a red-haired girl by his side, his arm round her, looking very happy.

'That's Chrissie. Just an old schoolfriend,' Paula explained quickly, turning the page. 'I don't know why I've still got that.'

And that was that. No further explanation but from the expression on Paula's face and the one on Matthew's when she asked about her, she knew that neither of them was in the mood for talking about the girl called Chrissie.

As for his sister Lucy … well, he would not be drawn on that either. Just to say that she died when she was thirteen and that it had devastated his mother.

'Have you a picture of her? I'd like to see her,' she asked, recalling that there were none about.

'I don't know what Mum did with them,' he told her shortly. 'Maybe she got rid of them. Maybe it was too painful to look at them. I don't know but please don't mention her. I know it's a long time ago but it's still raw for Mum. Christmas Day is a bummer because that was her birthday too.'

'What happened?' She needed to know so that she would not put her foot in it but Matthew just shook his head, expression closed and she knew better than to pursue it. She might broach the subject with Alan one day if ever she had the chance but she and her father-in-law were hardly ever alone and to this day the opportunity had not presented itself.

*

Getting in early from work, Nicola changed out of her work suit into shorts and tee-shirt before making a cup of coffee and, because they were having a good sunny spell, she chose to sit outside in the little patio area at the rear of the cottage. They must do something with the garden, she thought as she tried to relax, but neither of them were gardeners and she could not quite bring herself to employ somebody to do it for them.

They were reasonably comfortably off, for Matthew was doing well and had had a recent pay increase, but she did not earn enough in her opinion and that was a bore. She was used to getting what she wanted when she wanted it and having to save up for something was not coming easy to her. She could still wheedle anything she wanted out of her father but she was less inclined to ask for things these days because she did not want to embarrass her husband. Matthew – and she rather liked this – was an independent soul.

She had no idea how much her father was worth, how successful the Nightingale business was, but she knew that he classed himself as a very successful entrepreneur. He was a fine-art specialist and their trinkets or what her mother preferred to call *objets d'art* were sold on for huge profits and it still amazed her how much their clients were prepared to pay for stuff that would not be out of place in a skip.

It was her mother who had the eye, her father who balanced the books, but they both had the ability to entertain and woo the clients. Sometimes Nicola had the suspicion that there was an element of *The Emperor's New Clothes* about the whole set-up but she found it wise over the years not to argue with the choices her mother made, even if she personally found some of them hideous.

She had stuck to her guns, though, when it came to furnishing her own home, dismissing all advice, well meant but annoying, from her mother, and going for her own look. As it was a dear little cottage, she wanted to accentuate that, the furniture scaled down with a lot of floral cushions and throws, a look that delighted her at first but not for long. How had she ever thought that such a mismatch of patterns and colours would go together? It was like living in a kaleidoscope. Now that she had time to think more carefully, she wanted to go for a much edgier look, modern with a twist although she was not quite sure what that meant but it would not suit this house. Their next house would have room to breathe with space for sumptuous enormous sofas and she wanted a large bedroom with a separate dressing room and an en suite of course, instead of the tiny bathroom here with the fickle shower that was either a trickle or a torrent according to its mood.

After a year, this cottage by the banks of the river was beginning to depress her. It had seemed so sweet in such a romantic location when they first moved in, a little love nest, but now its quaintness was wearing thin and there was just not enough room. Close by the river as it was, there was a whiff of dampness about and it needed a lot of work to bring it up to scratch; it was also remote and she felt marooned here. What she would like was to have neighbours, a woman of her age, somewhere to pop in for a coffee and a chat, some woman she could talk to and grumble at. Ideally she would like to live in a village, somewhere where she and Matthew could make an impact, and she saw no reason why that could not be achieved sooner rather than later.

Men were such a pain, weren't they? Matthew was work-obsessed and all he could think about was his job and his clients and work-related problems. Aside from having a bash at cooking, he left all things domestic to her, so if she didn't do it then it simply did not get done, which was extremely annoying. Her mother had offered to pay for a cleaner but she could not get anybody to come as far out as this and, in any case, she did not care to have someone poking around when she was not here. She knew if the tables were turned and she was the cleaner and the lady of the house was out then she would certainly be unable to resist having a quick nosy around. Underneath the smart exterior she presented to the world, she knew she was a bit of a slut with sluttish habits and she did not want a cleaning woman finding out what lurked in her knickers drawer.

Matthew looked on this place as a hotel rather than a home, not interested in doing anything to it, and although she did not expect him to be some sort of do-it-yourself champion, she had hoped he would have got his finger out and done something during the past year. And another thing, when were they going to take a break themselves? No holidays were planned and they had left it a little late unless they did one of those last-minute things. She should just book something and sod him. Inform him when it was done and then he could not make excuses.

She would do that, she vowed, and also whilst she was at it she would ask an estate agent to call round to see what the place was worth now, if there was the remotest chance of them making a skinny profit if they sold.

She got up and, with the estate agent in mind, crouched down and picked out a few weeds from the narrow bed. Perhaps John, her mother's man, would agree to pop over for an afternoon and do something with it.

No, she would not be going on maternity leave any time soon, she had more or less said yesterday to Mr Gilbert. It had been a hilarious conversation when, discussing future events, he had not quite asked the question and she had not quite answered it. Apparently Emma's hints about moving back up north were becoming ever bolder and he felt it was just a matter of time. What would they do without her?

'You can rely on me long-term, Mr Gilbert,' Nicola said, tugging at her jacket so that he might notice just how smart and professional she looked. 'I can do this job standing on my head and I would love to be given the opportunity. Emma has been such a wonderful person to shadow and I have valued every minute spent with her.'

Was that overdoing it? Frankly Emma was a pain in the arse, a fusser and a flounderer, but she was not going to say a thing against the woman, not when for some daft reason Gerry Gilbert was half in love with Emma and thought the sun shone out of her large behind. Emma was one of those good-looking overweight blondes, her suits one size too small, but with ridiculously small feet that she squeezed into neat shoes. The size of her own feet, far too large, was the one thing she would change given the chance. Emma was a smiley individual loved by one and all, which did leave a sour taste in Nicola's mouth because she knew she was not liked half as much, but then people who spoke their minds seldom were.

Maternity leave? What a ghastly thought! She was nowhere near ready for all that and in fact, she was not sure she would ever be ready and, after a year of marriage, her mother was starting to drop not very delicate hints. She wanted to be a grandmother before she got too old to enjoy it and she was desperate to spend money on her first grandchild. He would want for nothing. Already, ridiculously, she was starting to think about possible schools for the as yet imaginary child, insisting that she would of course foot the bill. That was laughable because there was no way Matthew would agree to such a thing. He was proud of his school roots, of the ordinary inner-city school at which he had excelled, becoming head boy and the best performing student in his year which, coupled with a burning ambition to be the best, had led to his prestigious place at Oxford. If that school was good enough for him, then something of a similar vein would be more than good enough for his child.

Paula had not said a thing about children, never dropped

the slightest hint, at least not to her but then their relationship was not close. To her, Paula always seemed one step removed, awkward with her, keeping something from her, smiling on the surface but not within. Maybe she had not mentioned children because she just assumed it would happen eventually.

If so, it was a dangerous assumption.

She did not think of herself as maternal, able so far to contain the cooings and mummy-like face contortions which the average woman seemed unable to avoid when confronted by a baby but, when she and Matthew talked about it in general terms, a far-off family, she did not tell him that she was so frightened about the whole messy business of giving birth that she could not contemplate it.

She hated needles, hospitals, the indignity and most of the all the agony. She had seen those women on television writhing about screaming their heads off and it scared the shit out of her. She was no good with pain and unless she could be knocked out completely during the process she was not going to put herself into that unenviable position – legs apart, pushing until the slithery thing slipped out all covered in blood and looking like nothing on earth.

No, thank you very much.

She could, she reckoned, put Matthew off the idea for a number of years yet. After all, a lot of women these days did not become pregnant until their forties so there was ages to go, and by the time she was approaching forty they would be set in their ways and probably decide that it would be much too much of an upheaval. By then, they would be doing well in their careers and they would have a home somewhere by the sea to be proud of. She would end up like her mother; comfortably off and able to afford whatever she wanted, content enough with her husband – although making do with him might be a better description.

Married barely a year and already the excitement had

dimmed, the thrill of being together all the time had fizzled out and they had settled into a routine, as she supposed all married couples did sooner or later. Sex with Matthew was good, as good as any she had experienced before anyway, and there was most definitely a spark between them.

She really did love him and she knew that other women must envy her for having such a handsome husband.

As to children, the jury was out. She supposed she might succumb sooner or later because it did not seem quite fair to Matthew to deny him a child, but just now the only person who would be remotely disappointed about the non-appearance of children would be her mother. But that was only because she wanted to be seen as a glamorous grandmother.

But she would get over it and it would save her a fortune in school fees.

Chapter Nine

ELEANOR WAS GETTING ready for dinner that evening on the fifth day of their holiday. They did not get back until late from the trip to Verona through the manic Italian traffic, which gave them a shorter time than usual to get ready. Eleanor liked to take her time – scented bubbly bath, a rest with her feet up, then time spent doing hair, nails and make-up – so she was not in the best of moods.

She was in two minds whether or not to make a complaint to that useless tour rep, who ought to be aware by now just how long the journey back from Verona took, and in addition ought to take into account the fact that some people would always be back at the coach later than the appointed time. There had been a sarcastic round of applause when the late-comers had arrived, but although it was good-natured – for after all they were on holiday – it just wasn't good enough and she made sure from the glance she gave them that the couple knew her thoughts on the matter as they scuttled past her.

Arriving back eventually and throwing them out of the coach, dusty and dishevelled, with barely an hour before their dinner reservation, was just not good enough either. However, on balance, she decided to give the girl another chance as she did not wish to draw attention to her. She was annoyed with

Henry, who had flirted outrageously with the poor girl as they waited in Verona for the last of their party to arrive at the coach station. It had been just a touch embarrassing as she was sure that Paula had noticed. What was he thinking of? The girl was younger than Nicola for heaven's sake. However, she was not going to make a thing of it because it was just his way and it was going nowhere. She and Paula had seen little of the men that day, only meeting up again back at the coach where she had stored away her shopping; some gorgeous silky items from a boutique in Via Mazzini.

'What on earth did you two do all day?' she asked her husband.

'What did you ladies do? Other than shopping of course.'

'We had a lovely time. We had lunch and a wander round. Paula loved it all.'

'I'm knackered. Alan dragged me all around the bloody place. He had a list of things he wanted to see. We went to an ancient church and the old Roman theatre and some museum or other and then we climbed to the ...' He touched his head. 'Can't remember the name but we did have a good view from there and then I persuaded him to stop for lunch and we finished off with a few beers and then afterwards we looked at some paintings and statues in a gallery.'

'That must have been right up your street.'

'Not our thing, darling. The only paintings I care about are those that you can put a price tag on. I don't care if I never set foot in a museum again but you can't keep him away from them. Don't leave me alone with him again. This is a holiday for Christ's sake.'

She laughed. 'At least I don't have that problem with Paula. Did you talk about anything else, though? Anything more personal?'

'Such as?'

'Did you talk to Alan about his daughter?'

91

'What daughter?' Henry was still out on the balcony, in his day clothes, acting as if he had all the time in the world. However, she knew he could be in and out of the shower, shaved and dressed in fifteen minutes flat if he put his mind to it, so she was determined not to nag him.

'Their daughter died and Paula won't talk about her.' Eleanor deftly applied her make-up, pleased that her skin was holding up, although she needed a good coating of make-up these days to look her best. She was very careful now with the sun so as to avoid that awful deep-tanned look that used to be so popular. She regretted the hours spent soaking up the sun when she was younger, frying herself to a light-golden colour, but the damage was done and she had to make the best of it. Thank goodness her hair was still as sleek and thick as ever and tonight she had decided to wear it up which was always a fiddle but worth it. 'I tried to get her to open up about it and I was only trying to help but she clammed up. From my experience it would help her a lot if she would talk about it to a sympathetic listener.'

'It's not the sort of thing men talk about,' he said, coming back into the room and sliding the balcony window shut. The noises from the coast road were immediately shut off and the silence was welcome, although the low buzz of the air conditioning was a constant irritation. Henry was still in no hurry, the leisurely way he was taking off his shoes exasperating her.

'You must talk about something when you are together, when you were between museums for instance.'

'We talked about Verona and Veneto if you must know. Old Al is quite the historian. He did well at school apparently and could have gone to university but his father wanted him to go into the family business so he was not encouraged. I got the impression it was a bit of a sore point.'

'I find that hard to believe.' Frowning, Eleanor reached for her dress and stepped into it, turning so that Henry could zip her up. 'Perhaps he's just saying that to impress you. Anybody can say that they could have gone to university.'

She gave up on finding out any further information about the daughter from Henry but she was not giving up on more probing of her own. She had chosen the wrong moment, that was all, and been rather ham-fisted. A gentler approach was called for. The obvious clamming-up had succeeded in arousing her curiosity, though, and she determined to find out just what had happened. Nicola knew very little about it either which made her think that there was something odd about it. How had she died? Had it been an accident? An illness? Suicide? The latter might explain the reluctance to talk about it although it was too awful to contemplate. 'Alan doesn't strike me as the university type,' she finished, admiring herself in the mirror.

'You wouldn't say that if you'd heard him going on about Verona. He's a dark horse, that one. I tell you, the man's a walking bloody encyclopaedia. He looked it up, he said, before he came because he doesn't like to come to a place half-arsed.'

'I bet he didn't say that.'

'Maybe not the exact words but it was what he meant.'

'If that's the case, then that will be where Matthew gets his brains from,' Eleanor said, smoothing down her dress and glancing pointedly at her watch. 'It's certainly not from his mother. Paula, sweet as she is, is hardly the smartest lady, is she? She was very keen to tell me that she knew about *Romeo and Juliet*. She knew all about it she said. I expect she's watched something on television about it for I certainly don't have her down as a Shakespearian scholar.'

Henry laughed. 'You are right there.'

'It's lucky for Matthew that he's got his father's looks as well as the brains.'

'Apart from the eyes. He's got his mother's eyes. Have you noticed her eyes?'

'Can't say I have.'

'People would pay a fortune to have contact lenses that colour.'

'Do you think so?'

She hesitated, rooting through her jewellery and deciding on a simple silver strand necklace. The dress was burnt orange, not an easy colour, and not only because it was damned difficult to get a lipstick to tone, but she had managed it. She watched as her husband disappeared into the bathroom and wondered if she should attach any significance to the fact that he had noticed the colour of Paula's eyes. It irked her that he had noticed. Men rarely noticed women's eyes unless there was a sexual attraction, unless there had been direct eye contact. She wondered if Henry would remember the colour of her eyes if anyone should ever ask him.

As to Paula's, they were without doubt the woman's best feature. A subdued mix of green and grey, most unusual, and if she was lucky enough to have eyes that colour she would accentuate them cleverly with discreet eye make-up. Paula did not seem to bother much with make-up, just a touch of the same old pink lipstick and maybe a smudge of foundation but she scarcely needed it because her skin was enviably smooth and wrinkle-free and, to Eleanor's irritation, she looked considerably younger than her years. Of course the fact that she was so alarmingly tiny helped. From the back when she was wearing flat shoes, she could pass for a 12-year-old.

She was not too worried. Paula was hardly Henry's type, although judging by that ridiculous flirting with that little rep today he wasn't so fussy these days. He normally went for tall, smooth, sophisticated women and she had turned a blind eye over the years to the little infatuations he had had. If you married a man as winningly attractive as Henry, then the odds were stacked against you. Sex, while all right, had never been that important to her, but a comfortable lifestyle meant a lot and Henry provided her with that. She did not think of herself as being entirely dependent on him for she could support herself if necessary. She had had what she regarded as a distinguished teaching career in linguistics and enjoyed it while it lasted, but she also enjoyed early retirement from that and now she seemed busier than ever with all the social engagements she had to attend as well as her charitable events.

She was chairperson – for her sins – of the Ladies' Luncheon Group as well as being a previous president of the local WI and various other things. She very much enjoyed her role as one of the senior figures of the community – What on earth would we do without you, Eleanor? – and she never regretted their decision to remain here when they might have moved nearer to London once upon a time. It made sense from a business angle but it was so much easier these days to conduct business from wherever you happened to be; you could do it from bed if you liked from your laptop and certainly do it from the desk in their office at home with the spectacular view of the garden. Of course, they had to keep track of the galleries where they displayed the paintings and the more unusual items, but they had people to look after them and it all ran smoothly enough. She always attended when they had little events when they might showcase one of their artists, for example; champagne and nibbles and homing in on the right people on those occasions: people with money to burn, people who might be persuaded to part with it if they thought they were making an artistic investment. Quite a number of people were putting money into art at the expense of shares and so on and that was why they were bucking the trend and business-wise doing reasonably well.

She knew that her lazy attitude to sex disappointed her husband, although she could fake it when she had a mind to, so she was not too concerned if he looked elsewhere. All the important ladies of the past had always turned a blind eye to their husband's infidelities and having a mistress was common practice amongst the aristocracy. Henry could take a mistress if he so desired but she rather thought he was getting past all that. The pretence would be altogether too much of a hassle for him because, naively, he was unaware that she knew of the previous liaisons that had all ultimately petered out. She had been extra sweet towards him during those little episodes, working on the assumption that eventually guilt would over-power him and he would end it.

He always had.

'Ready, darling?' she called out a little later, for they had agreed to meet up with Paula and Alan in the bar. Henry emerged looking quite perfect, adjusting the cufflinks on his shirt, nodding his approval at her as she did a twirl for him.

'Will I do?' she asked, holding up her face for a kiss.

'Do?' he said, his voice a purr. 'I should say so. You'll be the belle of the ball as usual.'

She followed him out. Compliments were lovely but sometimes she wondered if her husband was operating on automatic pilot when he said them. As they waited for the lift, she wondered what pretty little dress Paula had picked out for this evening and what Alan would be wearing too.

She found Alan a little intriguing especially after what Henry had said about him.

There was more to him than met the eye.

The rush to the bar verged on unseemly and she left Henry to it, taking a seat beside Alan, who had appeared without his wife. He was wearing smart casual and wearing it well and she thought it odd that medium-priced clothes should look so good on the men when, on the ladies, they mostly looked cheap.

'Is Paula all right?' Eleanor enquired as she and Alan found a seat in the corner. 'I thought she looked a bit peaky on the way back. Does she need anything?'

'No, thanks. She's OK but tired and she has a headache coming on and no appetite. She thinks it's the heat. She's sorry but she doesn't want us to make a fuss. I offered to stay with her but she wouldn't have it.' He tapped his fingers on the table, looking around as if checking where Henry had got to. 'Just a small thing, Eleanor. She gets upset if you talk about Lucy so would you please not ask about her again?'

'Goodness, did I upset her?' Eleanor clutched her necklace. 'I'm so sorry if I did but I only thought it might help if she wanted to talk about it.'

'It doesn't help,' Alan said in that matter-of-fact way of his. He was very direct and for the first time she detected something of a stubborn nature. 'We've found the best way to deal with it is to try to forget it.' He looked at her and she was the first to look away, disturbed by the glance for, the more she knew about him, the more attractive he became and she was not sure how to deal with that. If she was not a woman in her fifties, she would say she was developing a teenage infatuation for him. 'We can't forget of course, neither of us,' he went on. 'But we keep up the pretence to each other. Paula suffers from guilt and there's nothing I can say to make that better. We stay strong, have done for years, but not necessarily both of us at the same time if you follow what I mean.'

'I do. I do, Alan. It must have been horrible to lose your daughter. A daughter is so special to her father, isn't she?'

'Very special. She was my little princess. I know everybody says that but she really was. She struggled when she was born, a little fighter, and that fighting spirit stayed with her until ...'

It was the first time she had seen any emotion from the man and even now, even as he uttered those deeply felt words, he kept it under control just about, his gaze steady, eyes clear.

'You poor things,' she said, her hand so close to his that it very nearly moved of its own accord to touch and offer support. Perhaps he sensed as much, for she saw him look down at her hand and move his away just as her husband appeared.

'Bloody chaotic, it's like a rugby scrum at that bar even at those prices,' Henry said cheerfully, interrupting them just when there had been a window of opportunity for her to find out more from Alan. Blissfully unaware of the tension in the air, a tension that Eleanor was acutely aware of, one that you could pluck like a string, Henry handed them their drinks. 'Are you sure she doesn't feel up to joining us, Al?'

'Paula is resting,' Eleanor told him, trying to catch his eye so that she could give him the nod that he was to drop the subject. 'What did you think of Verona, Alan? Henry tells me you did some research about it beforehand.'

'I did. I knew a bit about it but I needed to know more. It's always been my ambition to go to the opera at the Arena.'

'Don't tell me you're into opera?' Henry asked. 'You sly bugger.'

'I do a spot of singing,' Alan said, the surprise remark dropping into the conversation like a thud. 'I used to be in a choir but it got too difficult finding time to get along to the practice sessions. I miss it, though. You should try it. There's nothing quite like singing to lift the spirit.'

'Is there no end to this man's talents?' Henry asked after a moment. 'You kept that quiet, Al. I didn't know we had a Pavarotti in our midst.'

Alan grinned, unperturbed. 'Not quite. You should hear me. But I would like to see the opera, especially performed at the Arena. It must be quite a spectacle. There's always something special about open-air theatre, isn't there?'

'Oh yes, we love the Minack Theatre over in Cornwall, don't we, Henry?'

'It's all right,' he said without enthusiasm. 'Sitting on rocks in the pouring rain is not my idea of a good night, though.'

'That was just on one occasion. When the sun shines, it's magical.' Eleanor shot her husband a despairing glance. 'If only I'd known you were interested in opera, Alan. It's not going to be easy to get good tickets now, not at this late stage but we could try if you like for later in the week.'

'No, that's fine. I'm not too keen on the opera that's on just now. Perhaps another time. I'm hoping I will persuade Paula to come back here, maybe next year. Isn't opera your thing then, Henry?'

'Hell, no. All that screeching gets on my nerves. I don't mind a decent tenor but those bloody sopranos set my teeth on edge.'

'Henry has no musical appreciation whatsoever.' Eleanor cast an annoyed look his way. The fact that Alan sang had rather floored her. She would love to hear him sing but not just now. 'I adore opera of course and I do persuade him to go up to London occasionally.'

'You only do it to be seen, my darling, and to have an excuse to stay in a smart hotel and buy a new frock,' Henry said with a short laugh that infuriated her.

'I do not,' she retorted but not before she had seen Alan's scarcely concealed smile. Did the two of them discuss their wives when they were together? She hoped not for Henry was not known for his discretion. She knew Henry thought her cold sexually and she hoped to God he had not said as much to Alan. It suddenly mattered that Alan should not get that impression.

She finished her drink and stood up, annoyed with her husband for that 'opera' remark and giving Alan a very warm glance just so Henry would notice. Henry might be a little taller and broader than the other man but there was something about Alan that, just at this very moment, made Henry pale into insignificance. 'Shall we take our drinks through?'

She caught the return glance Alan gave her before spinning round on her heels and making a beeline for the restaurant. She knew she looked her best this evening and she knew, without a word being said, that Alan had noticed. It was a long time since another man had paid her any attention, not in that way, and it felt good, even if it would never amount to anything, for if ever a man was happily married, it was Alan.

If there was a little swagger in her movement, a little feminine hip swaying, then so be it. She was hotly aware of that glance and knew exactly what it meant. It was a long time since she had flirted and it was rather fun and it certainly wasn't her fault if Paula was being a wet blanket this evening – headache indeed!

As to Henry … if he thought he was going to make love to her later tonight, he could think again.

After dinner, they ended up on the hotel terrace where a pianist was playing background music. It was a balmy evening, the heat of the day lingering still, although Eleanor was glad of the feather-light shawl draped around her shoulders.

'Do you need to get back to your room to check on Paula?' she asked Alan. 'It's fine if you want to do that. We don't mind, do we, Henry?'

'She'll be asleep by now,' Alan said. 'She's not a night bird. She sometimes goes off to bed by ten at home.'

'Good God, does she? It's usually midnight for us, isn't it, darling?' Henry said. 'And these days I can't bloody get off to sleep as often as not and no …' He stole a glance at Eleanor. 'I am not starting on sleeping pills. That is the kiss of death. Now, if you'll excuse me I'm off to the little boys' room and if you like I'll order us some of their special coffees on the way.'

'That would be lovely. Thank you.' Eleanor watched as he disappeared.

Alone with Alan it felt awkward suddenly.

'You look nice tonight,' he said at last. 'But then you always do.'

'Thank you.' It was not exactly a fulsome compliment but it warmed her for unlike Henry, this man meant it. It also surprised her for she knew it was not something he would have said had his wife been present.

'Paula's enjoying it,' he said and there was something in his voice that concerned her. 'I've been trying to get her to do this sort of thing for years but she's always been so against it. It's as if she's frightened of enjoying herself.'

'I can understand it. Not everyone enjoys travelling and she doesn't like flying much so it can be a bit of an ordeal.'

'Are you and Henry OK?'

'Yes, of course. What on earth do you mean?' She looked at him, startled, for it was a strange question.

'Sorry. I just wondered.'

'He's not the easiest person but we get on well enough.'

'How long have you been married?'

'Just over thirty years.'

'Same for us although it's a few years more. It's a life sentence when you think about it.'

'A happy one, I hope?' she said, looking at him and seeing a sudden wariness cross his face. 'You two seem very content together.'

'Do we? It's not been as smooth as you might think. Losing Lucy was a big thing, you know, and there was a time shortly afterwards when we talked about separating.'

'Did you?' She was genuinely astonished.

'It was the grief. It started to annoy me that she couldn't get to grips with it. She was in tears for weeks, no let up at all and it was getting to be impossible. I tried to be patient but I couldn't get through to her and it was a very difficult time. To me she was being selfish thinking only of herself and not me.

She never asked once how I was coping with it. She just left me to get on with it. It didn't seem to occur to her that I was almost out of my mind with grief.'

'You've dealt with it in different ways,' she told him. 'When something as terrible as that happens you are on your own. You can help each other through it but I've seen a lot of relationships disintegrate after a trauma so you've done well to hold it together.'

'Thanks.' To her surprise he reached across the table and took her hand. 'I can talk to you, Eleanor, and that's a surprise because when I first met you I thought, this woman is going to be such hard work.'

'Did you really?' She felt the pressure of his hand, astonished that he had done this, and surely he held it a fraction longer than he ought, holding her gaze at that so that she felt quite hot and bothered as she caught sight of Henry heading back.

Alan had his back to him but there must have been something in her look that made him swiftly let go of her hand – although not before Henry had seen it.

She lay awake for what seemed hours that night thinking about it and the guilty look on Alan's face as Henry took a seat beside them.

You only looked guilty if you had something to hide.

Chapter Ten

PAULA CARRIED A small photograph of Lucy around with her, tucked into a pocket in her purse. Every time she opened the purse, it was a comfort to know that Lucy was there. Alan did not know about it so far as she knew, because he was not in the habit of going into her purse.

Of course she did not need a photograph because Lucy's face was deposited in her memory in a safe-box that she could open any time she wanted. More often than not, though, she thought of her daughter at a particular age, round about five years old when she had started school, her early promise of being a bright little girl fully realized.

There was a five-year gap between her children. It had not been their intention to have a gap as large as that but it was the way it happened and it worked well because when Matthew started school, she did not miss him as much as she might have as there was baby Lucy to care for. Lucy was premature but a good weight at just under six pounds and, from the beginning with her tiny hands and feet, she was destined to be just like Paula, challenged in height terms, with the same light-coloured hair which hairdressers always kindly described as fine when they clearly meant thin.

Lucy was the much-beloved baby girl but they tried not to

spoil her and Matthew was the big brother who adored her. There were spats of course as they grew older and she made fun of his girlfriends, embarrassing him and laughing about it, but it was all good-natured stuff. But when he went off to university, it was Lucy who probably missed him the most. She was thirteen at the time, still a lot smaller than all her schoolfriends but a popular, bright girl as, a little later than most of them, she started the process of maturing into a young woman.

'It's not the same,' she grumbled to her mother, 'with no Matty around.'

She was the only person who called him that. She would have gone far, would have followed her brother to university if she had anything to do with it. Alan, deprived of that opportunity, also had been dead keen on his children doing that. Nobody was more delighted than Alan when Matthew got his place because it was something he had been denied and to get such a fantastic offer as a place at Oxford had meant Alan had gone round for weeks bragging about it.

And so had she. They told his granddad the news but there was never a proper acknowledgement from him, not even a congratulations card, which would not have hurt him.

Paula, try as she would, had never got on with Thomas Walker.

'So you are the girlfriend?' he said when Alan first introduced her to him. 'There's not much of you, is there?'

She could tell from his expression that he did not think much of her and that, coupled with the anxiety of the occasion, made her more tongue-tied than usual although Alan had immediately taken hold of her hand and given it an encouraging squeeze. Alan's mother, frail even then, had welcomed her cautiously, but deliberately or not there had never been the opportunity to chat woman to woman as it were, so whatever her inner thoughts might be were never revealed.

It was his father's wish that Alan went into the family business, which was concerned with building and supplying specialized equipment to the maritime industry. It was a medium-sized business, moderately successful and the plan was that eventually Alan would take it over. But that was not to Alan's taste and the engineering industry was not something that fuelled his interest.

Alan's father was a bully, his mother a cowed little woman who did as she was told, and with the financial rug well and truly pulled from under his feet and no other means of supporting himself other than landing himself in enormous debt, Alan made the difficult decision not to accept the place he was offered. It was not Oxford but a good red-brick university and the course in European history promised to be fascinating.

'What the hell use is history?' his father had said, laughing at him. 'It's what's happening now that matters, not what people got up to God knows how many years ago. Anyway, I've not worked my socks off to get this business up and running to have my only son turn his nose up at it. You need to get a grip on reality, son. We can't all be astronauts.'

It was all very well being stubborn and Paula understood because Thomas Walker, Alan's dad, was an awkward individual who obviously had been as lukewarm about her as she was about him. Sometimes she wished Alan had swallowed his stupid pride and gone into the business, because from all accounts it was booming, his dad still nominally at the helm although there was a manager now who ran things. Thomas was known locally within the business community, admired for his tenacity, if not entirely liked, brusque and offensive to the ladies as he often was – it was something of a miracle that he had not been done for sexual harassment – and he had a finger in several business pies these days, still working a bit even in his late seventies. They heard on the grapevine that he had diversified and moved into property-developing a decade ago, and now owned a few houses which he let out to students. It was no secret and somehow or other Thomas made sure that they were drip-fed the information with I-told-you-so high on his agenda.

With his long-suffering mother long gone, Thomas was Alan's only living relative, but even though the old man only lived over in Torquay, they rarely visited or spoke. Thomas's annoyance at his son's refusal to go into the business had festered and simmered and eventually reached boiling point, culminating in a huge row shortly after she and Alan got married. His 'You can do a lot better than her' had infuriated Alan. Paula, hating family rifts, had tried to smooth things over and for a while there had been an uneasy truce when the children were small and they had paid Granddad occasional visits. He paid them scant attention and her efforts were doomed to fail and the visits became less frequent and eventually, with no effort coming from him, they petered out. It was the last straw when there was no acknowledgement from Thomas when Lucy died or when Matthew married.

She could just about turn a blind eye to his grandfather not coming to his grandson's wedding but not coming to Lucy's funeral was non-negotiable and she would never forgive him that.

She would shed no tears when Thomas Walker popped off.

Alone in the hotel room, lying on the bed propped up by a mountain of pillows, Paula was feeling a little better as her headache eased. She simply could not have faced the palaver of dinner this evening with Eleanor still insisting on speaking Italian, which made for an uneasy situation with their waiter, who would have much preferred to conduct the conversation in his charmingly accented English.

There had been no communication from Matthew or Nicola, but since she and Alan had requested a news blackout then she could not blame them for the silence.

All in all, the holiday was going well. She had caught something of Eleanor's enthusiasm for Italy and its people and the boat trips across and up the lake were introducing them to the many different little resorts dotted round the lake. There was not a lot of contact with the other people in the tour group but that was because the four of them were so obviously a little unit, and because Eleanor was a bit off-putting nobody had dared butt in. Amongst the group, though, Eleanor was definitely the one who stood out with her easy elegance and Paula had not failed to notice the looks other women cast her, reading their minds and knowing they were asking themselves how the hell she did it and, more to the point, what she had spent in order to achieve it.

So long as she pretty much agreed with Eleanor, it was all right. After all, the woman could not help it if she happened to be tall and slim with lustrous hair, something Paula yearned to have. Alan loved her as she was, and it was silly to be dissatisfied with yourself when there were others far worse off than you, but it was doubly annoying when you tried your very best to look your best and didn't always manage it and yet somebody like Eleanor always got it right. She was the sort who would look enchanting wearing a paper bag.

She had not yet got round to telling Alan that she had been offered a promotion at work to shop manager. It had been on the cards in the card shop for some time, because she was by far the longest-serving member of the team and knew the ins and outs of the job, despairing sometimes of the way the junior staff treated customers and not afraid of speaking out when that happened.

The promotion would mean a pay rise, which would be welcome, but it also involved more responsibility and that was why she was hesitating about accepting it. She knew both Alan and Matthew would tell her to go for it but she had seen what additional responsibility and the related stress did to people and that was why she was considering it carefully before she accepted. She was not the ambitious sort, more than content to just do the job as well as she could, and she knew that with the promotion would come meetings with the other managers in the group and the constant worry that her shop was under-performing and slipping in the company sales charts.

Although she was flattered to have been asked, she was not going to do it. In fact, she wouldn't even mention it to Alan, for what was the point? What he didn't know he couldn't worry about. Yes, the extra money would be nice but it wasn't worth making herself ill.

Getting off the bed, she padded barefoot across to the window. There was nobody in the pool and the blue water shimmered and glinted, moving restlessly as the sun lowered in the sky. There were streaks of pink there, so yet another fine day was promised for tomorrow.

She wondered what was happening back home and hoped Alice had not lost the key and was remembering to move the post from behind the door. Alice was scatty and forgetful and for a moment, she wondered if she should give her a quick call to remind her.

Forget it.

She pushed the anxious thought from her mind.

She was hungry now, but she could not turn up for dinner late so she would have to stay hungry. Alan had offered to stay with her, forego his dinner but she wouldn't hear of it. 'Don't let her get to you,' she had said, meaning Eleanor. 'Whatever she says, it's just water off a duck's back.'

'Don't worry. I can handle her,' he told her with a smile. 'She's a softie underneath.'

Now, why did she find that remark so disturbing?

Back home, Alice next door picked up the mail from Paula's

mat and took the letters through to the table in the kitchen. There were a few circulars, some junk mail but amongst them a serious-looking letter in a stiff white envelope, which she placed to one side with the other proper letters so that Paula would not throw them out by mistake.

She was not being nosey, not really, but she did notice that this newest letter was from a solicitor because the address was on the back.

She hoped it was not bad news.

Chapter Eleven

MATTHEW NORMALLY ATE lunch at his desk, a quick sand-wich and a coffee from the machine in the corridor if he was lucky, but that day he had decided for some reason – call it fate if you will – to take an hour off as he had an appoint-ment over in the South Hams area later in the afternoon; a potentially exciting commission from a client with big ideas and the money to make it work. It was just the sort of thing Matthew liked to get his teeth into. He liked to give the clients as much time as they needed, so he would not be clock-watching and would probably end up being late home and he had warned Nicola of that. It was her day to cook, but she was not the least interested in cooking so he was not building up his hopes too much and he suspected that an M&S ready meal would be awaiting him. He did not mind too much because he had not married his delectable wife for her cooking skills, rather because she was so delectable.

The honeymoon was over, very much so, but he had never expected marriage to be a bed of roses and he knew that they were well-matched. His beautiful wife was fiery and quick-tempered and he was just the opposite – freezer chilled – so there would never be a big explosion between them. He knew from the start that he would forever be the calming influence in their relationship. He had sussed out her faults from the beginning as she had probably done with him. He had known from the outset that she was a bit of a snob and spoilt, but she couldn't help that, being the only child of parents with money, and of course they wanted the best for her and they had given her the best. She probably realized too that he was defensive about his own background, feeling sometimes that he had to make excuses for it, which was unforgivable.

However, reining Nicola in was proving hard work and now that the cottage had lost its charm for her, it was an uphill struggle trying to convince her that they could not yet afford the house she craved. It was beyond them in financial terms and even though they were saving something each month, he reckoned they needed to stay at the cottage for at least five years before they could consider moving onwards and upwards.

It was a cool day, but as he strolled down to the Hoe away from the bustle of the shopping streets, the light sea breeze made it seem even cooler and he was glad of his jacket. The seagulls swooped and screamed and the sea was choppy and unappealing, faintly green but mainly grey. Amongst the ships in the distance, a large navy ship was ploughing through the waves and he felt that pride in his home city – the ocean city – that he knew and loved. Perversely, because at eighteen he couldn't wait to get away to Oxford, he had missed the place when he was away, missed the smell of the ocean, the screech of the gulls, so maybe if you were born close to the sea, it did seep somehow into your blood. He knew he had once warned his mother that he wouldn't be around here forever, but now that he was married and Nicola had her job at the hotel, he doubted he would be tempted to move. Perhaps you needed to leave a place before you really appreciated it for what it was worth.

He was not greatly interested in history as his father was,

but as he finally reached the Hoe he paused before the bronze statue of Sir Francis Drake standing there proudly on his plinth looking out to sea. The sea never changed. It would have been every bit as choppy in those distant days as it was now and he was reminded of just what an achievement that had been, that circumnavigation of the globe, something not easily undertaken now, let alone then, and there was always the story of the bowling match of course, which probably never happened but made for a good story anyway. Call the man what you want, a pirate maybe, but if he had lived today he would still have been a man to be reckoned with, a man with a good head on his shoulders who managed to keep it there by staying on the right side of his Queen through such turbulent times. Apparently the first thing he asked when he returned home after his voyage was 'Does the Queen still live?' It was odd to think just how inaccessible people were in those days, away for months without any means of communication when nowadays you felt vulnerable if you left your mobile at home.

Sinking into a contemplative mood, Matthew stood there a while, his eyes scanning the murky grey horizon. He should come and stand here more often, but when you lived so close to a place you never got round to it. You couldn't get away with living in Plymouth without knowing all there was to know about Francis Drake, although the man himself had spent a good deal of his childhood over in Kent. He remembered being taken on a school trip to the nearby Buckland Abbey where as a grown man Drake lived for a while, and standing there with his mates in the Great Hall on the very same floor that Drake stood on. There were monks buried beneath that floor as well, which had sent a shiver through the girls in his class, but aged ten he was more concerned with having a day off from school and messing about than listening and regrettably it had all gone in one ear and out the other.

His grandfather's business was in marine engineering but

like his father he had no particular interest in that either. That didn't stop a twinge of guilt that he hadn't seen the old man in years and that his granddad had never met Nicola. They had sent a wedding invitation but it was never answered.

It only took one person to hold out a hand for the other to grasp.

Perhaps it was up to him to do something. Maybe he should make an effort to build some bridges, for old Thomas Walker was not getting any younger but just now he had other things on his mind and the effort seemed too much. Family rifts were a pain and he couldn't help thinking that if Lucy was around she wouldn't have stood for it. He was surprised too that his mother seemed to have given up so easily, although he knew that she had half-expected the old man to turn up at Lucy's funeral and at his wedding.

'Luce …' He murmured the name to himself, surprised at the emotion that buffeted him suddenly as sharply as the sea breeze. Something in the breeze, something in his head, murmured 'Matty' and he looked round, startled. It had happened a few times since her death, a sort of peculiar filial communication, but it was not something he talked about to anybody, least of all his mother. She blamed herself for Lucy's death and nothing would change her mind.

His little sister would have been properly grown-up now, maybe married, maybe a mother herself and that would have made him an uncle. He wondered if she would have got on with Nicola or if they would be daggers drawn, but it was all hypothetical now – and what the hell had brought all this on?

The mood passed and he pulled back his shoulders and walked briskly on.

There were a few visitors about but as he wandered down towards the Barbican, he decided to have a bite and a coffee in a café. It would be nothing elaborate but the idea of eating a sandwich on a bench somewhere did not seem too good an idea as storm clouds were thudding in at speed and it was getting chillier by the minute. It was going to pour down soon. The smaller yachts were bunched together in the harbour, tossing a little as the water buckled beneath them, masts tinkling, and on the swing bridge by the Marine Aquarium, lights were flashing as it lifted to accommodate the sails of a vessel making its way into the safety of the harbour.

He and Nicola usually dined at one of the smarter establishments here in the city or somewhere out in the country when they had an evening out. He was not too familiar with any of the cheaper eating places, but in a crowded side street he found a reasonable-looking café with a good-enough-sounding lunch menu and made his way inside.

'Sit wherever you like,' the elderly waitress informed him, looking surprised to see him, and he did that, wondering at once if he had made a poor choice as the place was practically empty. As he settled at a table set for three, the bell tinkled and the door opened again and a woman came through.

A woman in her thirties with red hair chopped into one of those messy in-styles the smarter set were displaying these days, a woman wearing skin-tight blue jeans and a cream sloppy sweater, a woman wearing very little make-up, a woman with a striking face and anxious eyes.

Scanning the room she stopped dead when she saw him, did a double-take as he did, hesitated as he confirmed it with a nod, looking as if she might well make a run for it before managing a shocked smile.

'Well, fancy seeing you here,' she said. Matthew had half-risen from his seat, going towards her prepared for a social kiss, but he was too late for that gesture as, with a now rueful smile, she took a seat opposite.

'Hello, Chrissie,' he said, so shocked that for a moment he could not even summon up the momentum to reach for the large menu the waitress was handing them.

'The specials are on the board,' she said, eyeing them both a little accusingly. 'I'll give you a few minutes.'

After fourteen long years they needed considerably more than a few minutes.

Chapter Twelve

Paula was so glad to be home.

The last two days on holiday had dragged, to be honest, because in her head she started the countdown to being home. She thought she had packed well, but she was starting to run out of things although she could of course buy something from one of the cheerful colourful markets that Eleanor had taken her to. She hesitated because she knew that the abundance of flowing cotton dresses that looked wonderful here would not look quite so wonderful back home and she would end up stuffing it in the back of the wardrobe and never wearing it again.

It was so beautiful in the hotel by the lake being waited on hand and foot, soaking up the sun on the terrace. They had visited quaint villages with their terracotta and pastel-coloured houses and steep little streets. Paula had loved being on the lake, staring into the crystal-clear water and listening to those beguiling Italian voices. She had no idea what they were saying, but even the mundane sounded fantastic. As for Alan, he was lapping it all up, and saying that they needed to come back here because there was so much he did not have time to see.

For both of them then it was as close to heaven as you could get.

And yet ...

For one thing, the amount of food – delicious though it was – the sheer amount that she was consuming was beginning to have an effect and she was starting to feel bloated. She had eaten more than enough of those delicious Italian ice-creams served in tall glasses, served by elegant dark-haired twinkly-eyed waiters who knew just how far to go in the flirting stakes with middle-aged Englishwomen.

And so, on the final day, she would have much preferred a simple bowl of chicken soup and a roll to that last meal on offer in the splendour of that dining room. Eleanor was wearing a new dress purchased from the market, a sherbet-lemon colour that looked good on her, and she was wearing her hair long and loose, her bare shoulders bronzed and glistening. Rotating her dresses now, Paula was back to the first one she had worn, her tan not so pronounced as she took care in the sun. Henry let Alan choose the wine that evening – big of him – and Alan had chosen well, looking intently through the list as if he knew something about it and giving her a sly wink as he finally made the choice.

It was a good meal that final evening with Eleanor on good form, more relaxed than usual. It was Eleanor and Alan who did most of the talking. Henry seemed content to sit and listen and make occasional comments and she was happy too to sit there quietly, for when Eleanor shook off her abrasive cloak she was capable of being an amusing and entertaining dinner companion.

It was an early start next day, back to the airport in Milan and then, before they knew it, they would be home. She could not understand it, this desire to be home but, once she was on the plane, and then with Eddie in the car, the relief when they finally turned into the street was immense. She could even feel the tears pricking her eyes as Alan, understanding, squeezed her hand.

The street was bathed in summer sunshine, a more delicate summer sunshine here, and the house was blessedly still there. In one of her dreams on holiday it had burnt down and she had awoken in a sweat, crying out because Lucy was trapped inside. Often, in her dreams, Lucy was there somewhere, but always just out of reach.

She trusted Alice of course to keep an eye on things whilst they were away, but even so, Alice was not around all the time and she was deafer than she admitted, so if burglars had taken it upon themselves to do the worst, Alice wouldn't have heard a thing. She felt a vague excitement as she put the key in the lock and saw that everything was just as she left it.

Eddie helped them with the bags but refused to come in for a cup of tea as he had to get on. Alan treated him, giving him a bit extra to what they had agreed on, and they sent him on his way, relieved in fact that it was just the two of them because once Eddie got started on his naval adventures, you never heard the last of it.

It felt stuffy and she opened all the windows to let some fresh air in and put the kettle on and sat down for a while in the lounge before she so much as thought about the business of unpacking and washing the dirty clothes and putting everything away.

Alan, who was back to work the day after, rushed upstairs to check his emails and so on and she, with one more day off still, looked forward to sorting out everything later. Oh, the bliss of being able to sleep in her own bed tonight. The bed in that hotel had been all right, but there was nothing quite like your own bed and your own sheets and pillows.

And when had she become middle-aged?

Alice, bless her heart, had bought in some basics: milk, bread, ham and a packet of chocolate digestives so they would not starve, not immediately. She intended to go out shortly and buy Alice some flowers to go with the Italian biscuits and she already had a thank-you card to go with it, from their shop's luxury hand-printed range of course.

The post was sitting on top of the kitchen table neatly divided into two piles; proper letters and circulars. It was totally mad the amount of rubbish that came through that letter box.

She started to open them.

A week on and it was all looking back to normal, the holiday fading already in her head, and, although she had spoken on the phone to her son to break the long silence and tell him that they were back and to give him the other news, she was delighted as ever when he turned up on the doorstep. He was on his way home, he explained, and couldn't stop for long. They hugged each other and he held her tight a moment.

'Did you have a good time, Mum? You look well.'

'It was lovely. I like Italy and your dad was most impressed. We might go back next year, on our own. Did I tell you we went on a coach trip all around the lake, just the two of us? Eleanor had been before and didn't fancy a long day out so they did something different.' She hesitated because she didn't like to criticize the Nightingales, not to Matthew. 'We enjoyed that day, stopping off at all these little places on the way, and it was nice to have some time on our own. We sat beside a lovely couple from Bolton on the coach and we exchanged addresses. Mind you, I don't suppose we'll ever get up there. It's too far but they said they love Devon so ...'

Matthew laughed. 'You've set yourself up there, haven't you? You'll have them staying for a week if you're not careful.'

'It doesn't matter. As I say, they were very nice. A bit older than us with grandchildren.' She took a breath and looked at him. 'What did you think about your granddad dying?'

'I was sorry to hear that. It was a bit of a surprise.'

'You can say that again. It was a shock. We didn't even know he was ill, Matthew. Can you believe that? What does that make us look like? As if we didn't care. Nobody told us that he was dead. I don't know who went to the funeral. He was in a nursing home and we didn't know that either. I thought he was still at home. Stubborn old so-and-so, he should have told us or somebody should have told us. If I know him, I bet he told them not to tell us,' she said, knowing she was getting in a state, but that's what it had done to her, coming out of the blue as it did.

'I would have gone to the funeral if I'd known,' Matthew said.

'Would you? He didn't come to your sister's,' she said bitterly and then, running an agitated hand through her hair, 'Sorry. I shouldn't say that. And yes, I suppose I would have gone too if I'd known. As to the money, well, I feel terrible at taking his money but what can we do? If we refuse it, it will just go into the government's pot so we have a sort of duty to accept.' She was still trying to justify it to herself and this was the best she could come up with. 'I'll make sure you and Nicola have some of it of course. It's going to be much more than we'll need and you need the money now because we don't intend to pop off for a while yet.'

'Don't be daft. It's yours.'

'I hope he did care for us at the last and I'm sorry we didn't go to his funeral. But somebody should have told us. I would have gone to visit at the nursing home. I really would. We might have been friends again.'

'You were never friends.'

'That's true.' She raised her eyebrows. 'He never liked me, Matthew. He always said I wasn't good enough for your father.'

'He was wrong there, wasn't he?'

She smiled at that. He was a good son, but she had been doing some serious thinking since they heard the news. 'We've all been stupid and stubborn and it wasn't worth it, was it?

Families should stick together whatever happens. Me and your dad ...' she hesitated, not sure whether to tell him. 'We had a tough few months after Lucy died and it could have gone wrong for us but we stuck it out. Well, we should have done the same with your granddad. We should have kept in contact with him.'

'Stop beating yourself up about it. Just take the money because that's what he wanted. I'm glad for you, Mum. Have a good spend. You can move house now if you like.'

'I know and we should do it before we get any older.' She sat down at last, having fussed around her son from the moment he came in. He looked tired and a bit worried and she hoped everything was OK with him and Nicola, but it was more than her life was worth to ask.

'I've something to tell you,' he said, putting his cup down.

'Nicola's pregnant,' she said at once. 'Oh, I'm so glad for you both.'

'No. She's not and we have no plans there.' His smile was a touch forced. 'The thing is ... guess who I met up with the other day?'

'I don't know. Male or female?'

'Female.'

'Young or old?'

'Youngish.'

'Dead or alive?'

They laughed. They had played this game a lot, one of the games they played when the children were small and they were on a car journey.

'Give up.'

'Chrissie York ... she's not York any more but I don't know her surname now,' he said. 'She's back in town and we had lunch together. We couldn't avoid it because we both happened to be in the same café but it was all a bit awkward.'

'Chrissie? Well, I never. How is she these days?'

'Very well. She's had her hair cut.'

'That's no surprise. It is ... let's see ...'

'Fourteen years.'

'Is it really?'

'She teaches English.'

'Does she now? That's a surprise.' She didn't think Chrissie bright enough for that, but perhaps she had been a late developer. She smiled, determined not to say anything detrimental about the girl who was now a woman. She had never said anything against her when she and Matthew seemed so tied up together and she wasn't about to start now. 'Let Matthew find out in his own time' had always been her motto, but in the event Chrissie's sudden departure had put paid to all her concerns. 'Does she still talk for England?'

He smiled. 'You bet. She never drew breath.'

'She's married, then, if she isn't York any longer?'

He nodded. 'She's married to a pilot and she has two children and she seems very happy. They live in a house in Surrey and the house is worth close to a million. The kids are at private school and she has her own car and her husband plays golf and they go on two or three holidays a year, an exotic summer one and a winter skiing break. They're just back from three weeks in the States. They travelled business class so they must be rolling in it, or maybe he gets a staff discount. I wouldn't know.'

'She did have a lot to say.' Paula sniffed. A bit too much, in her opinion, a little hint there of over-egging the pudding, for surely it wasn't the done thing to do too much in the way of bragging. 'That must have been a surprise for you. What is she doing down here?'

'Visiting her mother. Her mother's been living back here for the last year and this is the first time Chrissie's had time to visit. She's not so good.'

'Who? Mrs York?'

He nodded.

'I'll go and visit her if you like, if you can find out her address,' she offered, although as quickly as the thought struck her she wished she had not said it. 'Not that we knew each other that well in the first place so ...'

'It's not a good idea, Mum. Leave it. After all, if we hadn't met by chance the other day I wouldn't know that Chrissie had ever been back, would I? She certainly wasn't going to try to get back in touch with me, not deliberately. It was pure coincidence that we happened to be in the same café.'

Paula sniffed. She did not believe in coincidence and knowing how devious Chrissie had always been she wondered about that, but again she was not going to stir things up. 'Married with children, eh? And a teacher. Married to a pilot at that.'

'Long-haul. His schedule is frantic but she has help in the house and had a nanny when the children were small. The boy is at boarding school and the girl a day boarder.'

'Did she ask after me and your dad?'

The hesitation was minimal, telling. 'Yes. She asked me to pass on her regards.'

'Thank you. Does she know about Lucy?'

He nodded. 'She did know. I don't know how.'

'It made a few of the nationals ...' Tucked away in the middle pages somewhere, just a paragraph with a photograph of course, another little tragic story for journalists to lick their lips over. 'So I suppose she might have read about it, although I don't recall a card from her or that mother of hers. Not to worry, and she's done well with her life, then, from all accounts.'

From her accounts, that is, and she had always reckoned that Chrissie York played light and loose with the truth. Some of the things she came out with about the father who had left them, for instance, had been hard to swallow and Matthew, a young boy in the first throes of first love, had always been a soft touch. Alan too had always been taken in by Chrissie, but then she had such a doe-eyed innocence about her and Paula had always felt a bit mean that she had forever harboured doubts. 'Was she pleased to see you? You must have had some catching-up to do.'

'Yes, we did. I don't think she was that pleased but she could hardly walk out when there I was. It was good to see her but it's unsettled me. I wish I hadn't. I thought I'd put that behind me. I had this memory in my head and she's different now. She's not the same person any more. She's not the girl I knew.'

'Of course she's not, so maybe that's good, then. I know you were upset at the time but I think we make that first-love thing more important than it is. I can remember my first proper boy-friend. He was called Jack. Jack Evans and—'

'Don't start, Mum,' Matthew interrupted her. 'I know you mean well but I wish I hadn't said anything now.'

'Will you be seeing her again?'

He shook his head. 'No. She did suggest it and wanted to exchange phone numbers, but I didn't think it was a good idea.'

'Did you tell her that?'

'I just avoided doing it at the end, hoping she wouldn't notice. I wanted a clean break, Mum. I don't particularly want to see her again. You can't go back, can you? That's why I don't go along to those school reunions. It's just upsetting because, good or bad, we've all grown older and moved on.'

'No, and you're right, it's not a good idea. I expect it was nice to see her again but leave it at that.'

'She's meeting her husband and the kids off the London train later in the week and they're all spending a few days here with her mother before they go back home. But she's not going to be introducing me to them and I don't particularly want to see them either.'

'Be honest. You don't want to see him. The pilot.'

'Well, no I don't.'

'In case you get jealous?'

'Have you been listening? I'm over it, Mum. It's taken a long time and I have to admit I've thought about her more than once, but I'm over it now. And I'm married too.'

'Yes, you are,' she told him with a smile, very nearly tempted to tell him, after all this time that she, and perhaps more importantly his sister Lucy, had never liked Chrissie, manipulative being the one word that sprang instantly to mind. 'So just forget it and concentrate on making Nicola happy.'

Chapter Thirteen

HE WAS NOT cut out for this cloak-and-dagger stuff, Matthew thought, as he lurked in the station. Lurking was not something he was comfortable with. He had checked the board and the time, and people were starting to arrive to pick up passengers from the imminent London train, which was on time according to the board.

He was skiving. Well, not exactly, but it felt like it. He had a meeting in an hour and nobody questioned him leaving the office. He was putting in a lot of extra hours lately because of the work he had secured over in the South Hams for their millionaire client. It was exciting stuff and he had been given very nearly a blank canvas to work with, his brief being to come up with something spectacular for a large barn conversion. It might prove to be a tussle with the local planning department, but he loved a challenge like that and the ideas were coming at him thick and fast.

So, he ought not to feel guilty about taking a little time off. He never meant to come here to the station but it was as if he couldn't help it and he had found himself walking from the centre of town through the subway under the roundabout towards the station. It was chaotic as usual as stations always are, which was good because it meant it was easy enough to merge into the background. What he did not want was for Chrissie to spot him, because although if that happened he would claim he was meeting a client, he knew she would not believe that.

Fourteen years might have passed, but she could read him like a book as he could her. There were so many things they had not said to each other in the café, but they were both thinking them because memories such as the ones they shared could never be completely erased. After the shock of meeting her again, he had seen through the constant chatter, the idyllic life she was supposed to be leading, and seen it for what it was worth.

Chrissie was not as happy as she was making out.

He had not been strictly honest with his mother for, since the meeting in the café, he had thought about Chrissie quite a bit, thought of what might have been if she hadn't moved away at such a critical stage in their relationship. Yes, he knew they were kids themselves at the time – although of course they thought they were grown-ups – but he also knew that it had meant something and that she would always have a place in his heart. And although he thought he had put the whole sorry business to the back of his mind, it had resurfaced like an unexploded bomb when they met again.

Just for the briefest moment it was as if she had never changed. She was now a woman, a mother, but underneath it all she was still the girl he had loved once upon a time, once upon a time being the crucial point because, as they chatted, or rather as she chatted and he listened, he realized with something of a shock that he no longer did. Love, that teenage angst type of love, was gone. Too much had happened and there was far too much water, a great gush of it, under the bridge. She was the same but somehow quite different. And so was he.

She had indeed chatted non-stop, rummaging in her bag

halfway through, looking for photographs but suddenly zipping it shut.

'They're in my other bag,' she said, shoving this one down on the floor.

She blushed as she said it and he knew that was not true, for he had caught a glimpse of some photographs before she shut the bag. She probably had second thoughts about bringing him up to speed on her life by showing actual photographs of her family. It was best that they remain in shadow. He did not carry any photographs on his person, he noted in some surprise, deciding that he should at the least have one of Nicola tucked away somewhere, but then men were not like women. They didn't produce photographs at the drop of a hat.

'What's your wife like?' Chrissie had asked and he had given a careful description as if he had been asked to do so by the police. Kept it to appearance only, nothing about her character, her quick temper, her slow attention span, the way she was already picking faults with the cottage that she had once considered perfect, the way she was putting off the question of children. They were still young, loads of time, but nevertheless he noticed a caginess there, an unwillingness to discuss it, and he felt they should have some plan for the future in place. Look at Chrissie, a year younger than he and she already had her family. Her eyes lit up when she talked about her children, whose names he had now forgotten.

He could not remember what he ate in that café that day, but he did remember in vivid detail the way they exited into heavy rain, forcing them to shelter in a doorway with just her small red umbrella keeping some of it at bay. She was not fooling him completely. He had noticed a sadness that ought not to be there, not in a woman who was supposedly so content, and he was uncomfortable because he thought he also detected a softening in those eyes when she looked at him.

'Is everything all right? You can be honest with me,' he

asked, having to squeeze closer as somebody else, half-drenched, shot into the doorway with them.

'Of course everything's all right. Why shouldn't it be?' she said, lips pursed, those grey eyes casting him the quickest of glances. 'Sorry this has happened. It did cross my mind that you might still be around but I thought it unlikely because you always said you meant to move away once you left university,' she said, speaking low, mindful of the person squashed near them.

It seemed like a criticism and he corrected her swiftly, saying that, although he had considered a job in London, this one had turned up and he had seized the opportunity. Perhaps, during the course of the conversation in the café, he might have exaggerated the importance of his position but after all the stuff about her husband and the fancy house and so on he had felt a need to do that.

'God, this is like the tropics,' she went on as the rain upped a gear.

It *was* like the tropics and the torrential rain ended a few minutes later as quickly as it began. And would you believe a watery sun came out. People emerged, shaking themselves like dogs, and walked by along the glistening pavement and they did too.

At the end of the street, their ways parted and they said all the right things, how nice it was to catch up and so on, but there were no farewell kisses. Faintly discomfited, he watched until she turned the corner.

He never expected to see her again.

And here he was, at the station, lurking like a seedy private eye. His mother was right, because he was just being plain nosey and he did want to see what this bloke, this bloody fantastic bloke who had given her such a good life, looked like. Chrissie had arrived at the station last minute and looking harassed. She was casually dressed, wearing the tight jeans that she seemed to favour and a skimpy cream top looking like a vest with something printed on the front of it. It was shapeless, thin material, and her bra straps, black at that, were showing. He never thought much about women's clothes but it did occur that Nicola would never ever wear a top that showed off her bra straps, nor would she wear a black bra under a light top. Nicola was like her mother, always beautifully turned out, and he realized that he took that for granted, never complimented her much on it.

Chrissie, without the benefit of the chunky sweater she was wearing before, was very slim, painfully so, and he wondered why on earth she had had her hair cut in that way when it used to be so gorgeous: long and a little curly. The husband, whose name he did remember – Marcus – wouldn't enjoy running his fingers through that ragged crop. He felt a stupid and irrational dislike of the man he did not know, the man who shared his bed with Chrissie, the father of her children.

He should forget this now and go before she spotted him, but it was as if he was rooted to the spot and he remained there. She was scanning the arrivals board and standing alone and he made sure he was half-hidden in the shop doorway, although she was much more concerned with looking towards the barrier now as the board read that the train had arrived, and a few minutes later the first trickle of passengers filtered through.

Within minutes, they were flooding through, the seasoned travellers just making their way steadily, the rest being met. There were hugs and cries of delight all around and he felt a stupid lump in his throat as he watched a young couple rushing towards each other and embracing, the man holding the girl tightly as if he was never going to let her go again.

And then, Chrissie was waving her hand and he saw a grumpy-looking man coming towards her accompanied by children. He was of average height but solidly built and was wearing jeans and a short-sleeved blue shirt and he had the confident swagger of a long-haul pilot. Matthew managed an inward smile, wondering quite why he was being so unjust to the pilots of the world, who were probably without exception great guys. This pilot was OK-looking, but losing his hair, Matthew noted with some satisfaction. As they approached each other, it was a surprise that there were no good-to-see-you hugs, at least not from him to her, although she dipped down to put her arms round the children.

He ducked back into the shop doorway as they passed by. The son, eight or so, looked very like his dad, with the same dark hair, the same sulky expression. The little girl, a red-head like Mum, was a couple of years younger and she was holding her mother's hand now and chattering away nineteen to the dozen – definitely Chrissie's child. To his surprise, they looked a bit scruffy, not the sort of people who lived in a house worth a million but that could be something to do with the travelling. Nobody looked at their best after a long train journey.

It was difficult to pin down quite why, but they would never qualify as the perfect family, if there was such a thing, for even as they passed close by, he heard the man saying something sharply to Chrissie and saw the look on her face. For a minute she looked, not exactly scared, but like a teenage girl told off by her dad, chastened but a touch defiant. It must be something to do with what she was wearing because they stopped a moment and, with face flushed, she adjusted her top and the bra straps as her husband looked on.

He could be completely out of order here of course and it was just a feeling but Matthew harboured no satisfaction in the knowledge that the wonderful marriage, the fabulous husband, was all in her head and that it wasn't as great as all that. He hoped it wasn't as bad as it looked and that it was just a normal up-and-down sort of relationship: but then wasn't his exactly the same?

He watched as they disappeared into the crowd, waiting a while to give them chance to get away before he emerged himself. He used the time to go into the shop proper to buy a newspaper and a bar of chocolate. And, as he paid for them, the woman across the counter smiled at him and he smiled back as he pocketed his change.

It was suddenly as if a great weight lifted off him.

Chrissie, the girl of old, was gone and that was finally that. His mum was right and it was high time he let boyhood fantasies go.

This time he would not pursue her further, he would not allow her to invade his head again as she had done time after time because she was the past and Nicola, his beautiful gorgeous wife, was his future.

Just now, as the sun broke through the clouds, and he hurried back to the office, the future seemed rosy.

Chapter Fourteen

NICOLA WAS HOME first and she was in a good mood. Her parents were back and the holiday had gone well, her mother said, with no major problems as her father had so pessimistically predicted.

She had talked on the phone with her mother and, as they were free on Sunday, they were going over to have lunch with them. Matthew had seen his mother recently and all seemed well there too. Matthew had a big commission at work and was working all hours, at the office and here at home in the little second bedroom that they had turned into an office. They both needed a break, but just now was not the moment.

Quickly, she unpacked the grocery shopping and laid out the things she needed for dinner. She was making an effort tonight, actually cooking it herself rather than relying on the good old standby, M&S. After all, she had something to celebrate and maybe before long there would be even more to celebrate.

At work, Emma had finally done it. She was moving – hurrah! – back up north, dragging her partner with her, and Gerry Gilbert had hinted as strongly as it was possible to hint that the job was hers for the taking although, worryingly, they were advertising it.

She needed this promotion, which would up her salary considerably, although annoyingly Gerry seemed as concerned as ever that she might let him down by going on maternity leave any time soon.

What was wrong with the man?

Had she not made it perfectly clear?

Dismissing him, she concentrated on the job in hand, peeling and chopping vegetables and finding she was actually rather enjoying it. She had a bottle of strong Aussie wine – sod it, it would do them no harm once in a while – and a bought lemon cheesecake to follow the main course.

She was sweetening Matthew up, preparing him for what she was planning this weekend. On impulse, she had arranged to view a house, a proper house, which seemed on paper to fulfil most of her requirements. It was deeper into Devon, better for both of them from the commuting angle, and it was in a village setting which meant there would be near neighbours. It was the very last house in the village, on the way out – or the way in: whichever way you looked at it. It was a solid, dependable sort of property, which would probably go to a London buyer as a second home used only sparingly, which would be heresy. It needed to be the main home, the family home, the forever home and just the thought of it was exciting and suddenly everything was looking rosy.

She had done some boring sums and concluded that, once she got Emma's job, the increase in her salary would be significant and they would easily be able to afford an increase in mortgage payments. However, Matthew was boringly inflexible about spending money that they did not actually have so a little seduction this evening would not go amiss either.

Hence the wine.

The phone rang, the landline, as she was making the final preparations for the meal. She had texted Matthew and was planning that everything would be ready about half an hour after he arrived home.

Wiping a hand on the tea-towel she was carrying, she picked up the phone and chanted her number.

'Is that Mrs Walker? Nicola?'

She did not confirm that, immediately thinking it was one of those infuriating calls about cavity-wall insulation or the like, but the woman did not sound as if she was in a call-centre environment and the next words confirmed it.

'I will keep this brief, but you must tell Matthew to stop harassing me,' she said. 'I'm sorry to ring you but it would be a waste of time talking to him about it. You know what men are like.'

She was stunned into silence but only for a moment. 'What the hell are you talking about? Harassing? My husband does not harass anybody,' she said, wifely hackles rising.

'Doesn't he? Then why was he stalking me at the station the other day? Ask him that. My husband is a pilot with a very short fuse and I warn you that if I were to tell him, he would take a very poor view of it. I am very happily married, Mrs Walker. We have two children at private school and we live in a beautiful part of the country and our house is worth in excess of a million.'

'Who are you?' Nicola was tempted to replace the receiver. A crank call, that was what it was. But the woman called her Nicola and talked about Matthew so she did not hang up. Her hands, though, felt suddenly clammy and she could not quite believe what she was hearing.

'My name is Chrissie. I knew your husband a long time ago when I lived in Plymouth but we lost touch when I moved away.'

She knew instantly who it was. It was the Chrissie girl in the photograph. The redhead.

'You two were schoolfriends?' she said, remembering what

Paula had said as she tried to make sense of this.

'You could say that, although it was a little more than that.' The laugh was annoying. 'I take it he hasn't bothered to tell you that we met up the other day. Your husband and I met in town and it didn't take long for me to realize that he has never got over me, not completely, and I couldn't believe it that after we said goodbye he then had the effrontery to follow up that meeting by coming to the station where I was meeting my husband and children off the train. Knowing he was there watching us took the edge of what was a very private reunion. He should be thankful that I chose not to mention this to my husband, as he would be incensed. He is a very jealous man.'

'Now just a minute ... I haven't a clue what you are talking about ...'

'Ask that husband of yours. I just want to tell you that I will not take kindly to it if there is any repetition in the future. Thank you and goodbye.'

And with that, she replaced the receiver.

She waited until Matthew was changed and they were having a glass of pre-dinner wine before bringing it up. Quickly she brought him up to speed with what had happened.

'You didn't tell me you'd met this woman,' she said, trying her best not to sound accusing.

'No, I didn't because it wasn't that important.' He was flushed with annoyance. 'I was in a café in the Barbican and she just happened to come in. I hadn't seen her for years but we recognized each other and we had a spot to eat together. What else could we do? The café was empty. We could hardly sit at separate tables. You didn't know her so what was the point of me telling you? I told Mum.'

'Is she unhinged?'

'Who? Mum?'

'Don't be daft. This Chrissie woman.'

'I don't know. Why?'

'It was just the way she spoke. Very clipped. Very precise. As if she was reading from a script. Very uptight.'

'She is a bit intense, but she seemed rational enough, although she was very keen to tell me how well she was doing.'

'She was keen to tell me that too. In about ten minutes she told me her life story. She is married to a pilot with two kids at private school and they live in a house worth a million. In excess of a million.'

They shared a small smile but hers rapidly vanished.

'Come on, Matthew. What were you doing at the station?' she asked quietly. 'And don't you dare tell me you weren't there.'

Matthew put down his drink. He could kill Chrissie for this. How had she found out his telephone number, for one thing, but then they were not ex-directory so it was hardly rocket science. What had possessed her to ring his wife, other than a desire to cause trouble between them?

'Look, I admit, I went to the station like she says but I was meeting a client off the train that afternoon ...' The lie – why? – was out before he could stop it.

'A client? Who? Since when do you meet clients at the station?'

He knew he was digging a big hole for himself, and how he wished he could retract the lie, but he had no choice but to bluff his way out of it.

'I do sometimes,' he said, not even convincing himself. 'Anyway, I most certainly was not harassing her.'

He followed Nicola into the kitchen where the table in the alcove was prettily laid with a little vase of freshly picked roses as a centrepiece. Knowing she must have been out in the garden hacking away at the rose bushes, knowing also the extent of her cooking skills, Matthew felt a great fondness almost overwhelming him as he viewed the efforts she had gone to. When she put her mind to it, his wife could really hit the mark.

What was all this in aid of? Was he missing something? It wasn't his birthday, her birthday, or their anniversary but she was obviously softening him up for something. Just now though, he was in trouble, with her trust shaken, and he needed to convince her that there was nothing in it. Could he get away with a change of subject?

'That smells good.'

'And so it bloody well should. I've been slaving over this stove ever since I got in.' Nicola was standing there, knife in hand and looking as if she might use it. Flushed, but that could be from standing over the cooker, eyes bright, hair ever so slightly frizzed; and she looked pretty fantastic. He nearly told her so, but that would go down like a lead balloon in the mood she was in. He was so lucky to have this woman, this exciting awkward, unpredictable, gorgeous woman. She might be all those things, but she was not sullen or sulky or miserable, not for long anyway. She was not perfect, but then neither was he and neither, he now realized, was Chrissie: the girl he had put on some sort of pedestal for years. Frankly Chrissie, the new version, was proving to be a pain in the arse.

He tried to advance towards her but she waved the knife threateningly so that he laughed because he could not believe for a minute she would use it.

'Don't build this up into something it's not. I love you, darling,' he said.

'And I love you, you bastard.'

'I admit I used to think I loved Chrissie but that was a long time ago and meeting her again made me realize that I don't any more. She was just a kid and now she's grown up and she's different. It was nice to catch up in a way but that's all. I won't be seeing her again and good riddance if all she can do is come up with this. Harassing her? Who does she think she is?'

Nicola put the knife down, picked up a spoon and took off the lid of a pan so that steam shot in the air.

'What were you doing at the station? And don't give me that crap about meeting a client either.'

'I admit I was curious. I wanted to see what this husband of hers looked like. I wanted to see what this marvellous-sounding pilot looked like, this guy who earns so much money that he can afford to buy his wife a house worth a million when all I can afford for my wife is this hovel.'

There was a little silence. She had her back to him but he sensed a softening there. 'It's not a hovel,' she said quietly.

'Isn't it? Anyway, I don't know why I did it but perhaps I wanted to get some closure,' he finished, wondering where on earth he'd dug that one up from.

'Oh, please, Matthew.' She almost laughed.

'It's true. I needed to see him. And now I have and I've sussed it all out. She made it sound as if she was living the dream and she's not. Not by any means. She's married but I don't think she's particularly happy. Not like we are,' he added carefully, smiling at her as she turned, and heading her way to put his arms round her. 'What can I say? I'm sorry that you had to listen to her and I'm even sorrier that I ever met up with her again. And I'm sorry that I can't afford to buy you the house of your dreams. We have to wait a while, my darling.'

She was busy now at the hob but she had relaxed and he did too. Turning, she gave him a rueful but forgiving smile.

'You are pretty wonderful,' he said. 'Husbands have been shot for less.'

'Don't push it, babe,' she said. 'I am simply giving you the benefit of the doubt because I happen to be in a good mood so I will forgive this barmy Chrissie woman. But, just think about it, she must still fancy the pants off you,' Nicola said, unable to hide a smile now.

'What makes you think that?'

'Because she wouldn't go to all this trouble if she didn't. She told me you had never got over her, not completely, when she means the opposite. She means that she has never got over you. It's obvious. Don't you know anything about women, Matthew?'

'Only that you are a race apart,' he said.

So, Chrissie had seen him at the station, not surprising because he was not James Bond and his attempt to stay hidden was pathetic, but why had she ignored him and why on earth had she called Nicola? Harassing her? Nothing was further from the truth.

Big mistakes had been made in the way he had handled this. He should have come clean with Nicola right away instead of keeping it quiet, because by keeping it quiet, it made it a secret and secrets between husband and wife were dangerous.

He vowed that, in future, he would tell his wife everything.

And later, he had to admit that his wife certainly knew how to choose her moment because he found himself agreeing to view a property at the weekend, one that sounded altogether too big and grand and far too expensive.

However, with all this Chrissie business looming large, he was in the doghouse and he needed to keep a very low profile for some time to come.

Chapter Fifteen

ELEANOR PUT THE finishing touches to the display of autumnal flowers on the side table in the hall. The mirror beside it doubled the impact and she stood back admiring the effect.

She loved autumn, even though it was the toughest season of the year in the garden. It was all to do with the dratted leaves of course, and the constant clearing-up, but John kept it all under control leaving her to enjoy the more leisurely jobs of pruning, trimming and cutting flowers for the house. This arrangement in a sturdy ceramic pot was predominantly orange and yellow with masses of greenery. She liked an arrangement to look as if it had just been thrown together in passing, when in fact it had taken all afternoon to get it just right. She had taken evening classes in floral display some years ago, but the woman taking the classes had been officious and patronizing and Eleanor decided that she knew most of what the woman was telling her anyway. She had a creative flair that was essential to the business, for Henry, even with his background in fine arts, was apt to miss things.

She was expecting Nicola for afternoon tea, a meal sadly neglected these days, but she liked the idea of tea and fancy cakes at four o'clock – how civilized – and Nicola looked as if she needed feeding up having lost weight recently. That, and a vaguely lost look, was enough to cause Eleanor to worry a little and she had confided in Henry, asking if she ought to make a mention of it, because she did not want to upset Nicola or to imply that she was in any way criticizing her. Like her father, Nicola was quick to fly off the handle.

Henry's opinion was that it was best left and that if anything was worrying her, Nicola would tell her mother in due course. She wouldn't bet on that, because they had never gone in much for the mother/daughter thing.

Content at last with the flowers, she scrunched up the tissue paper and carried it into the kitchen, checking that everything was on hand for when Nicola arrived. The tray was laid with pretty china cups and the little cakes on the cake-stand looked tempting and she hoped she might persuade Nicola to have at least one. It might only be her daughter she was entertaining, but that did not matter for she disliked letting her considerable standards slip. Lately, with Henry being in a mood most of the time, something to do with work that he was keeping quiet about, it was easy to forgo those standards, but she was damned if she was going to ask what was the matter with him. Like his daughter, he would no doubt deign to tell her in due course, although she was becoming increasingly frustrated with him these days, her willingness to forgive his past misdemeanours in a meltdown.

It was a chilly start to autumn and, going through to the sitting room where she had lit a fire, Eleanor reflected that on cool overcast days like today it was hard to remember those heady summer days, particularly the ones spent with Paula and Alan in Italy.

Henry had been proved wrong for, in her eyes, it had been an excellent holiday. Since then, they had not seen much of each other, although they took the Walkers out for dinner at one of their favourite hotels, following which Paula invited them to her home and, unable to come up with a suitable excuse on the spur of the moment, she had initially accepted only to pull out at the last minute, pleading illness on Henry's part.

'She'll see right through that,' Henry said when she told him that should anyone ask he was suffering from sickness and diarrhoea. 'Why the hell can't we go along? It won't hurt us, will it? Are you sure we're asked to the house?'

'Absolutely. The invitation was perfectly clear.'

'Oh, I thought they might book us into some country pub because Alan will want to treat us for a change. I've told you before that it upsets him when you insist on paying for every bloody thing. Or rather, insist I pay. Can't you see how he hates it? He's a proud man.'

'Nonsense. We can afford it and they can't.'

'Can't they? What's this I hear about an inheritance? They didn't mention it last time we saw them, did they?'

'No, they didn't. They were probably embarrassed. Alan's father died and I gather they've been left a few thousand or so which I suppose will be a lot to them.'

'Good for them. Even a few thousand is not to be sniffed at.'

'No, but it's hardly going to change their lives, is it?'

Since dropping out of the invitation on account of poor Henry's incapacity, she had heard nothing from Paula and, as time went by, she was disinclined to be the first to phone to check if all was well. She had made up her mind, however, that if another invitation was forthcoming she would have to bite the bullet and accept or risk an atmosphere for years to come.

She wished she could erase some of the things that had happened on holiday, particularly that night in the hotel bar when she and Alan had the heart to heart and he took hold of her hand. What man does that to another man's wife? It could be excused because he was emotional, talking about his dead daughter, but nonetheless she felt uncomfortable still at the memory. But they were bound together for the long haul, the four of them, in-laws, and there was no option but to put it behind her and make sure that in future she avoided a one-to-one situation with him.

Nicola was right. There was no need for them to be in each other's pockets.

Or in each other's hearts.

Sitting waiting for Nicola, Eleanor looked happily round the room, her favourite room in the whole house. She had help with the original design but over the years, she had added her own touches and having recently redecorated, she thought the present scheme was the best ever. They had used some of their collection of special pieces brought from France but they were flexible and Eleanor was not overly precious about any of them. She would happily hand any of them over if a client particularly wanted something on those lines and they had nothing in the shop stock.

There was Nicola at last. Eleanor did not rush to get up, watching as her daughter parked the car and climbed out carrying that over-large handbag of hers, casual in jeans and short padded jacket. Her hair was just scrunched back in a ponytail and even from a distance she looked tired.

Was she pregnant? Maybe she was waiting for confirmation before she told her, although Eleanor thought it unlikely as Nicola had never been one for holding onto a secret. The cottage had been up for sale for a while but they had withdrawn it when there was no interest, and the last time Eleanor had visited she was just a little concerned at the state of it. Matthew was no do-it-yourself man, but surely they could get somebody in to attend to the myriad of jobs that needed attention. It was the details that mattered and she thought she had drummed that into her daughter. She had always been a touch slovenly and without Eleanor on hand to pick things up, without cleaning help, her daughter's home was starting to look like a tip.

With a sigh, for how on earth could she say anything without getting her back up, she got up, adding another tweak to the flowers in the hall before opening the door just as Nicola arrived in the porch.

They hugged each other and Nicola took off her jacket, discarding it casually on a chair beside the hall table. Pointedly, Eleanor retrieved it and hung it up.

'Do I need to take my boots off? They're not muddy,' Nicola said, indicating the knee-length boots into which her jeans were neatly tucked.

'You'll be more comfortable without them,' Eleanor said with a smile. 'They are very smart, I have to say. Where did you get them?'

'That shop in Wadebridge.'

'Do you want to borrow some slippers?'

'No. I hate slippers.'

She unzipped and tugged off her boots anyway, leaving them parked in the hall, and followed her mother into the sitting room.

'Do you want tea straightaway or shall we have a chat first?' Eleanor asked, taking in her daughter's pale face and tired eyes as she sank onto the enormous off-white sofa, tucking her legs up and yawning.

'Chat about what?' Nicola asked warily. 'You haven't got me here to give me the third degree, have you?'

'Of course not. What an idea!' Eleanor laughed although it had crossed her mind that before this afternoon was out she would get to the bottom of whatever it was that was bothering her. 'We don't get the chance very often to get together so we should do it when we can.'

'How did your trip to France go?'

'Very well. We got some super stuff.' She was not going to admit that the trip had been fraught, that Henry had been in a foul mood throughout and that he had been insufferably mean when it came to spending money. He said their normal hotel, the one they usually stayed at, was fully booked and they stayed instead for the two nights at a substandard one. 'How's Matthew?'

'Fine. I think ...' she added, lips pursing so that Eleanor had the confirmation – if she needed it – that something was wrong.

'Don't you know?' The question was sharp and she saw Nicola jerk her head and chew on her lip, a sure sign, a child-hood sign, that she was fighting hard to keep her composure. She could not remember the last time she had seen her daughter in tears, other than a few joyful ones at her wedding – which frankly she had her doubts about. 'Have you two had a tiff?'

'Not exactly, but it's all a bit flat at the moment. It's the house thing, Mum. I want to move and I just can't get him to do it. That one we viewed a few months ago is still on the market so we could get it for a song if only I could get him to see sense. I can't stand that place a minute longer. I hate it. It's getting me down. It's freezing now, like living in an igloo, so what the hell will it be like in winter?'

Eleanor smiled. 'Igloos are very warm, I understand.'

Nicola frowned. 'You know what I mean.'

'Don't I remember you saying how romantic a coal fire would be? You've got a beautiful inglenook fireplace. Use it. You'll be wonderfully warm.'

'I've tried it and I can't be arsed with it.'

'Nicola, please, I do wish you would watch your language.'

Her daughter gave her a look. 'It takes forever to light it and then it's smoky. It stinks the place out and it burns logs like nobody's business. And you are only warm if you stand right beside it. Give me a gas fire any day or best of all underfloor heating.'

'Do stop complaining. If you are like this at home it's no

surprise that Matthew is fed up. Being petulant will get you nowhere. You have to learn how to handle the men, darling. Look at me and your father.'

Nicola gave a little snort. 'You two are a fine example.'

'Meaning?'

'Oh, come on, Mother, surely you can't imagine that I was oblivious to what was going on between you two when I was growing up? Please don't insult me by pretending that you have the happiest marriage ever. Perhaps Alan and Paula can lay claim to that, but not you.'

'We have been very happily married,' Eleanor said stiffly, then seeing her daughter's face she relented. 'All right, it's not been all roses and romance but I learned how to deal with it. With his little … dalliances.'

'Dalliances?' Nicola laughed. 'Daddy and his dalliances. Did you always know?'

'I …' Eleanor was lost momentarily for words. It had never been spoken about but she guessed that, as Nicola grew older, it was pretty obvious what was going on under their very noses. So there was no point in denying it, not now. 'It took a long time the first time to acknowledge it, but after that I always knew the signs to look for. But that's something you have no reason to worry about. Matthew is not your father.'

'No, he's not and I love him and I can't imagine life without him but it's all gone a bit pear-shaped.' Impatiently, she wiped her eyes where a few tears were now lodged. 'Not getting the promotion was a big blow, Mum. I should have got it. The woman they've brought in is absolutely useless. I feel really let down. I think Gerry Gilbert only gave her the job because she's had an hysterectomy so she's not going to be going on maternity leave any time soon. I think I could sue him for discrimination because he has this extraordinary attitude to women of childbearing age. He thinks we're all on the verge of having a baby and that's why I didn't get the job.'

'Oh dear. I'm sure that's not the reason. You are very young still and perhaps you need a little more experience. I remember when I was in line for head of department at school and I didn't get it. It is very disappointing but it happens and it usually happens for a reason. Matthew was very sympathetic, wasn't he?'

'Yes, but he wasn't that concerned. He would be delighted if I took maternity leave.'

'Then why don't you?' she asked gently. 'Take a break. It's time, surely.'

'I can't get pregnant. I haven't said anything to him because I don't want to worry him but I'm off the pill and I'm still not pregnant. What if I can't have a baby? What then?'

'You've changed your tune,' Eleanor said. 'The last time we spoke you told me that I had better not hold my breath about grandchildren. You more or less said you weren't going to bother so what's changed your mind?'

'I don't know.' She bit her lip and looked like a child again. 'I'm not going to have a baby just to please you and Matthew. I want one too and when Simone asked me to be godmother, I was really pleased, and baby Eli was a little dream at the christening. I held him and he took hold of my finger and ...' she shrugged, looking shamefaced. 'I don't know what came over me.'

Eleanor nodded, not surprised. 'I'm afraid it does rather creep up on you.'

'In the house that I want ...'

'You're not still on about Tall Trees, are you? You have to accept that you are not going to get that property, darling.'

'It's still on the market. Anyway, there is a room overlooking the garden which would make a wonderful nursery. It also has a dining room and a lovely conservatory, a proper old-fashioned one, not one of those tacky things. And it's got this big terrace and a lawn and a separate little herb garden. If

I'm pregnant then we will have to move. There's no room for a cat, let alone a baby in the cottage.'

'Oh, Nicola, when will you learn?' Eleanor flinched. 'I want a grandchild more than anything but I do not want you having a baby for the wrong reasons. You have to want one, darling, really want one. If not, then don't bother. The problem with you …' She hesitated because she was about to admit that her parenting skills had not been the best. 'We've spoilt you. You are too used to getting what you want and I think Matthew is quite right. You must be patient about the house. And if that's what all this is about, getting a bigger house, then it's nothing to worry about at all. You will sort that out.'

Eleanor tried to get herself together, her daughter's distress catching at her, but even as she made to get up to go over to her, Nicola waved her back impatiently as if to say 'Leave me alone.' She had always been like that, never one for the sympathetic reaction, never one really for a cuddle. 'And you should count your lucky stars that he's not having an affair for believe me that is ten times more difficult to cope with. I am not going into details but it has been far from easy. Let me tell you that Matthew is a good man and he works hard and he does not deserve a grumpy wife. So, it's tough but you must snap out of this mood, darling, or you will drive him away. And then you will only have yourself to blame. As to becoming pregnant, you haven't been off the pill for long and it takes a little time sometimes so it's early days. You'll be pregnant before you know it, but I do want you to be sure about it.'

'I think I am.' Nicola managed a rueful smile. 'I'm scared stiff at the thought of having it, but you managed it, didn't you?'

'And millions of other women before me.' Eleanor sighed with relief. So it was probably just stage fright after all, and deep down her daughter wanted a baby as much as the next woman. 'Relax and it will happen and don't bother Matthew about it. I know he will be thrilled when it does happen.'

'He's very preoccupied. I catch him sitting there staring into space.'

'Men often are preoccupied. It will be work-related. It always is. Do you want your father to talk to him?'

'What about? That's the worst idea ever. I wonder if it might be something to do with that Chrissie woman. Do you remember me telling you about her?'

'Yes, but it blew over, didn't it? You haven't heard from her since?'

'No, I haven't but has he? You don't suppose he is seeing her on the quiet, do you? You don't suppose that he's meeting up with this woman whilst her husband is away flying his plane?'

Eleanor laughed. 'I don't suppose that for a moment. Don't be suspicious, whatever you do. Talk to him. Tell him you're worried. Ask him what is worrying him. Do you want me to ask Paula to have a word?'

'I wish you wouldn't. We don't talk, if you must know. She irritates me too much and I'm scared I'm going to say something sooner or later that upsets her. So it is best if we stay clear of each other.'

'I get on well with her.'

'Do you? I suppose it will do no harm. See if she can throw some light on it. I don't know if Matthew talks to her or not.'

'I don't understand. I thought you and Paula got on well together.'

'Oh, come on, Mother. She's never liked me and made that fairly obvious. The fact that I've met the Queen is my only saving grace in her eyes.'

'Wait a minute.' Eleanor paused. 'You are wrong. Paula adores you, darling. You're just like a daughter to her. She lost her real daughter and you've made up for it in a small way.'

'No I haven't, and please don't patronize me, Mother.'

'Don't do anything in haste. Don't upset Matthew too much.

Play it very carefully. If I were you I would do absolutely nothing.'

'And there speaks the voice of experience.'

'You did ask for my advice.' Eleanor felt a tightness in her chest. 'You can be very brusque sometimes, Nicola, and it does not become you.'

'I'm sorry.' Nicola sighed, reaching out for a cake and taking it carefully from its paper case. She stuffed it in her mouth and chewed on it, dropping a few crumbs and shaking them off onto the carpet. 'The trouble is, I don't want to know in case he really is having an affair. Suppose he's meeting up secretly with that Chrissie woman?'

'Will you stop that? What have I just said about suspicion? Now you are being neurotic. That was all explained away. It was a schoolboy crush and it's over and he's not going to see her again.'

'Yes, but suppose he is. After all, she must still love him, even though she's supposed to be the happiest married woman on the planet. Seeing him again that day must have rekindled it for her and seeing him at the station really set things alight.'

'Nicola. For goodness' sake, get a grip. You are building things up out of all proportion. You have to pull yourself together,' she said briskly, knowing that those were words you should never ever use to the people she had occasionally counselled, but deciding that they were appropriate here. 'Your honeymoon is over and life is full of ups and downs. This is just a little blip and you will get over it.'

'I won't be able to stay with him if he has been shagging another woman.'

'Nicola!'

'Sorry but I'm not like you. I suppose it was different in your day,' Nicola said, regaining her composure. 'You stuck together no matter what.'

'I'm not that old and I know plenty of people who divorced,'

Eleanor said, stung by the 'in your day' as if she was a hundred. 'I am just saying that you are in a stupid panic about nothing. Jumping to conclusions is very unwise.'

'I know, but I don't know what to do. I feel bloody miserable.'

'It's probably just your hormones.'

'Oh, please. That is supposed to explain everything, isn't it? But you may be right because I'm getting myself worked up about the baby. I want to be knocked out, Mum, when I give birth. Can I request a Caesarean on the NHS or will I have to go private?'

'Stop worrying. Good heavens, Nicola, I hope I won't have to put up with all this nonsense for the next nine months.'

'But you're my mother. You know about these things,' she said, looking so childlike and leaving Eleanor quite bemused.

'I'm glad you've told me all this, darling.' She smiled, genuinely pleased because they were not that close, the two of them, and it delighted her that when it came to the crunch Nicola thought of her. 'As you are so concerned, I will speak to Paula but I want to do it face to face not over the phone. If – and it is a big if – if he is having an affair, then I can't believe she doesn't know about it because she and that son of hers are thick as thieves.'

'Can I stay here tonight?' Nicola asked. 'I need some time on my own.'

'No, you cannot.' Eleanor decided the time had come to be brisk. 'You will go home and act as if there is nothing wrong. Carry on as normal. Consider what is the very worst that can happen. Confront that and you will be fine.'

'The worst thing is that he leaves me for this other woman. What if she loves him so much that she leaves the pilot and the kids just to be with him?' Nicola spoke in a small voice, totally changed, and she was shocked to see the transformation, which she did not like. Where was her confident, sassy daughter, who like herself did not suffer fools gladly, the daughter who normally could give as good as she got? She wanted that girl back, because just now she looked in danger of becoming a snivelling wreck and it was so out of character that she was quite alarmed. 'We've only been married just over a year. What will people say? What does that make me look like?'

'Is that all you can think about? What other people might think?'

'No it's not, Mother, and you know it. I happen to love the bastard to bits and I don't want to lose him and it's taken something like this ...' She moved to put her plate on the table clattering it down as she did so. 'It's taken something like this when I think I might lose him to make me realize how much I want him to stay. I want him to move with me to the big house when we can afford it and if we never can then we'll have to find some way of doing up the cottage so that it's bearable there. I am not giving up on him, Mum. I want to grow old with him, like you and Dad.'

'Thanks for that.' Eleanor tried a small smile. 'Leave it with me. I'll have a little chat with Paula. I find she's always more than happy to speak to me.'

Chapter Sixteen

Paula received a summons in writing from Her Ladyship to meet in town for lunch and a catch-up.

'Why didn't she send an email like anybody else?' Alan said when she showed him the short note stating a time and place. 'Or phone you?'

'Because she knows I'm upset still about her making an excuse not to come over for dinner.'

'Henry was ill, wasn't he?'

She huffed at that. 'You'd believe anything. I've been waiting for her to make a move. Perhaps she's going to apologize.'

'Will you accept it?'

'I don't know.' She smiled. 'I might and I might not. I might make her sweat a bit first.'

'My God, Paula, you've changed,' Alan said and he didn't sound exactly pleased. 'Once upon a time you wouldn't have dared say anything to upset Eleanor. In fact, once upon a time, you would hardly have dared to say a word in her company. Coming into money has certainly changed you.'

'Don't say that. It doesn't sound right. You should be pleased I'm standing up to her. I am every bit as good as she is and so are you, Alan. You are worth ten of Henry.'

'Only ten?' He laughed shortly.

'I have to start telling her what I really think. I've been biting my tongue too long when I'm with her and I'm getting too old to be such a wimp. The truth is I've always been lacking in confidence,' she went on thoughtfully. 'It was your father, you know,' she told him. 'When I heard him say that I wasn't good enough for you, that you could do better than me, it had a big effect on me. At that time, I think I was just starting to feel more confident, breaking away from Mother and planning to get married to you. I was feeling good about myself and then I heard him say that and it knocked all my confidence because my mother thought much the same about me. She didn't think I would ever make much of myself. She told me I would never be an actress, said I wasn't good enough and I believed her. It's a bit late in the day now but I'm finally starting to believe in myself. Does that make sense?'

'Have you been reading one of those self-help manuals?' he asked incredulously. 'I've never heard you talk like this before but I tell you this. I wish my father was here now. I wish he could hear what you said just now. Because he would have to admit that he was wrong. Mind you, I have to admit that I loved you as you were. I loved taking care of you, looking after you, loved being protective towards you.'

It was a disturbing thing for him to say, talking about love in the past tense as if, now that she was starting to shake off all those old inhibitions about herself, he now had doubts.

'You do still love me, don't you?' she asked, searching his face so that he gave her a much-needed hug and told her that of course he did.

He had had to be prompted, though, to say it.

She knew that she alone was responsible for the change in herself, that somehow Eleanor and her reaction to Eleanor was part of it too, so it wasn't all about the inheritance. It happened on holiday. It was Juliet's balcony that did it for she realized then that in fact she probably knew a damned sight more about that Shakespeare play than the lady herself.

A lot had happened since their holiday and she knew that Eleanor must be aware of their changed circumstances, although there had been no acknowledgment from her. In fact, things had been a little strained since the holiday. There was one dinner out together at a fancy hotel in Cornwall in early August but the way Eleanor had snubbed her invitation to come along to her home for a meal hit hard. Alan had suggested that they invite the Nightingales to a restaurant of their choice, somewhere in Plymouth, but she had thought that it was time they entertained in their home. In a sudden surge of domestic pride she was damned if she was going to be ashamed of her own home, which was her little palace and she wanted to show it off.

It was the fact that Eleanor made a fool of her that offended her most. She would not have minded so much if she had refused the invitation straight off but to say yes and then back out at the last minute with a lame excuse was unforgivable. Much to Alan's amusement, she had even bought a new rug and curtains for the dining room and some new dishes, some smart white ones, and she had planned the meal for a week beforehand because, although she considered herself a competent cook, she was not a confident one. Poor Alan had the same meal three nights running until she was sure she had it right.

Alan had sorted out some wine, something good from Waitrose, a couple of bottles at that, and she got the loft ladder out and rooted through some boxes to find the fancy wine glasses somebody had bought them for their silver wedding. And then she got some flowers from a florist's and the woman had picked out a lovely big spray for her to arrange at home. She dusted and polished all day long and the house was so clean you could perform an operation on the kitchen worktop.

All that fuss and then, at the last minute, Eleanor had the brass neck to ring up and say that Henry was incapacitated and could they possibly rearrange at a later date.

She could forget that.

The inheritance was not through, not absolutely, but because it was just a matter of the solicitor sorting it all out for them, they had agreed that they could spend some of their own savings, which now seemed like a drop in the ocean compared with the amount they were going to get from Thomas. So she had been on a shopping spree and treated herself to a few new outfits.

For the meeting in town with Eleanor she wore a navy suit – knee-length pencil skirt, fitted jacket – teaming it with a colourful scarf and spanking heels, her hair newly coloured and a little longer because she was trying to grow it into a new style. She arrived in town in plenty of time because the last thing she wanted was to be rushed and flushed; because Eleanor would be neither.

Catching a glimpse of herself in a shop window she reflected that it was astonishing what a difference good-quality clothes – and high-end shoes and handbag – did for the morale. It was almost as if she was now playing a different character and it felt liberating. She was no longer Little Miss Dowdy and she felt so much more confident in herself, a new woman no less; Alice next door had remarked on it, telling her she looked a million dollars. She was going to treat Alice to a little something when the money came through, but it would have to be carefully thought out because she didn't want to look as if she was showing off, so she must not overdo the gesture.

After some thought, they were going to take the plunge and move house although she was not entirely sure she wanted to. It was sort of expected now that they had come into money and it would be exciting to furnish and decorate a new place, and they had started looking for somewhere on the outskirts. She was not yet ready for a bungalow but a small detached with a garden would be ideal.

Today she avoided going past the card shop even though there was absolutely no reason why she should. After all, she had resigned and because she did not want to leave them short-staffed, she worked the full notice and the big boss had turned up on her final day and presented her with a little gift and a nice farewell card of course, one of their pricier hand-made numbers. There were a few tears because she had enjoyed working there, although in a way it was a relief because it saved her the bother of making a decision about the promotion.

She avoided the shop because for some daft reason she did not want them to think she was somehow checking up on them, seeing how the new woman was getting on, the one who had replaced her: a snooty individual with purple nails to whom she had taken an instant dislike.

It was no longer her problem and money was no longer a problem either, which took some getting used to. It made her feel just the teeniest bit guilty for surely one or other of them, Alan or his father, could have made an effort during the last few years, one or other of them could have got down from their high horse and tried for a reconciliation. She was not a blood relative and it had been ultimately up to Alan to do something about it, but that remark his father had made all those years ago about her not being good enough had hit home and hurt him every bit as much as it hurt her. It was no use feeling guilty and she reminded herself that they had not seen hide nor hair of Thomas Walker at Lucy's funeral, or at Matthew's wedding, and the old so-and-so could have got off his fat behind and come to see them.

She supposed, in Thomas's eyes, by leaving Alan the lot,

including the surprising number of properties he had accumulated, Thomas would feel he had redeemed himself. By accepting it and not telling the old fool to stuff his fortune, they had more or less forgiven him although they had to assuage their conscience in some way and they would be setting aside some for the local charities that they already supported.

Paula glanced at her watch before making her way to the little Italian restaurant, much-praised locally, where she was meeting Eleanor. As of old, an attack of nerves overtook her, but she must not allow herself to show it. She was on stage now, playing the part of a confident contented woman.

She had an idea what this might be about, although she hadn't said anything to Alan. She had seen her son recently and although he told her all was well she knew it was not. Sons could not fool their mothers. Matthew was working too hard these days and he should relax a little because, at his age, there should be much more to life than work. That business with Chrissie had upset him of course, for who liked to be accused of harassment particularly when there wasn't a word of truth in it? She had wormed that story out of him after Nicola had rung her and started to ask questions about Chrissie, before eventually coming out with it.

She might have known.

She had always been neurotic, had Chrissie. She wished she had seen Chrissie again because she was one step removed from the whole situation and she would have known straightaway whether or not Chrissie was happy in her life. In fact, she would have asked outright because Chrissie had always responded to the direct question. Chrissie York had been one of those worryingly intense young girls and nobody had been more relieved than she was when she moved away and was no longer a threat to her son's happiness. She would have wrung him dry, that young madam, and it took a mother to know it. However, her son was a romantic and there was nothing wrong with that, but she was still at a loss as to why he had gone to the station that day when he had told her he was not going.

That had been a mistake and a half.

After their shouts of delight and meeting-hugs, Eleanor bit her tongue, stopping herself from making a remark about the way Paula looked, for it was truly a remarkable transformation. Her whole demeanour was different, as if the well-cut suit, the good shoes and the lovely handbag – not to mention the flattering scarf – had given her a much-needed confidence boost. She was altogether more poised and she walked differently, although that could be something to do with the spiky-heeled shoes.

'You look nice,' Paula said, giving her the opportunity to respond.

'I like your new hairdo,' she murmured, irritated though, because today of all days – and uncharacteristically for her – she was having a truly awful hair day, a fact which she was certain Paula noted. Threatening to be late, she had in the end given up on it and just scraped it back into a ponytail. She had missed her last hair appointment and a few grey hairs were beginning to show, which was doubly annoying. 'It suits you,' she added, in for a penny in for a pound.

'Thanks. I'm growing it. It's taking ages,' Paula said as they settled at the reserved table towards the rear, a table where they could conduct their conversation without fear of being overheard. 'How are you, Eleanor?' she asked, slipping off her leather gloves. There was a new ring on her right hand, Eleanor noted, and it was not costume jewellery either.

'Very well, thank you. And you?'

'Fine.'

Good. Niceties out of the way, then.

'Good afternoon, ladies.'

The waiter appeared, handing them the menus and there followed some consultation before they both settled on lasagne and two glasses of wine, red for Eleanor, white for Paula.

'I shouldn't. I'm driving, but one glass will do no harm,' Eleanor said, mindful of Paula's expression, but then she was married to a driving instructor who absolutely never ever drank when driving. She was beginning to realize that Alan Walker was a man of principle, which was of course something to be admired. Her own husband took no notice whatsoever of the rules of the road, overtaking on blind bends and what have you, and it was a miracle he had never been involved in an accident. 'Look, Paula …' She hesitated but it needed to be said. 'I'm so sorry if I upset you when I had to cancel dinner, but Henry was really poorly, honestly, and it couldn't be helped. I hope you didn't think I was making an excuse.'

'That's all right.'

Eleanor waited, half-expecting another date to be suggested but with none forthcoming she carried on. 'Nicola came by for tea the other afternoon.'

'That's nice for you. I haven't seen her for a while.'

'She was off-duty and we don't often have the chance to catch up. You know, the mother-and-daughter thing.' She stopped dead when she realized just what she had said but Paula seemed unperturbed, remarkably cool today, distant too. Hastily, she moved on to chat about other things; their husbands' health, the weather, the autumn/winter fashions at Marks & Spencer, but it was a relief when the food arrived with a flourish and after the usual fuss with accompaniments, the waiter left them in peace.

Eleanor took a sip of her wine. 'It's only one glass,' she repeated, Paula's look making her feel guilty. 'Don't tell Alan and I shall be very careful on the way home,' she added.

'Glad to hear it.'

'It's strange that you don't drive, Paula.' Eleanor smiled. 'I suppose you two would argue terribly if Alan tried to teach you.'

'I've never felt the need, although it's never too late, is it? Do you know you've got me thinking? I shouldn't rely on Alan all the time. All the ladies drive these days, don't they? Some of Alan's clients are older than me so why on earth am I waiting?'

'It would give you so much more independence if you can drive yourself around.'

'Yes it would. I might start lessons, not with Alan, though. You're right about that. It would be a mistake. This is delicious, by the way.'

'Yes, it is a good attempt, although it doesn't compare of course with the real thing. Do you remember our lunch in that restaurant in Venice? They were proper lasagnes, weren't they, not cheap imitations.'

Paula glanced round hurriedly, for it was hardly the thing to say within hearing distance of the waiting staff, but fortunately for once Eleanor's ringing tones seemed not to have been overheard.

Paula did remember the restaurant in a side street off St Mark's Square, remembered too, how Eleanor had taken charge, fluttering away in Italian as usual, remembered too the glance Henry shot her, the glance that said more than a thousand words, the glance that told her what she already knew, that he was willing if she was. It was a very popular restaurant, not the usual tourist haunt but one that the locals enjoyed, so that for once Eleanor's knowledge of the language was most helpful. It was crammed to capacity, so much so that they were squeezed together on a table that was barely adequate for two.

Somehow she and Henry had ended up side by side on the bench with the other two opposite and she was very aware of his leg against hers – and surely an additional pressure as she caught the sideways glance that was nothing to do with the lack of space. It made her blush but it was so damned hot in the very middle of the restaurant that she hoped her pink cheeks would be put down to that. She was wearing a sundress in palest blue with tiny shoestring straps and she was realizing a little too late that it was not providing enough bust support, so she had to hitch up the straps from time to time.

Sitting there on the bench in that crowded restaurant, at first she thought it was a mistake, that it was not intentional, but when Henry dropped his hand down to her thigh and stroked it, that was quite different. It took a huge effort to remain seated for she was very effectively trapped there. She knew full well that Henry was aware that she would stay silent rather than cause a scene and mortify both Alan and Eleanor. She could not believe it. How dare he? She was happily married, had been for years, and she had never in all her married life looked at another man, not in that way. Why should she when Alan satisfied her very nicely when it came to all that?

She very nearly blurted it out to Alan that evening but she did not want to ruin the rest of the holiday and she was not sure how he would react. Good heavens, the four of them were in this relationship for the long haul with their children married to each other, so perhaps a discreet stepping-back might be the best option. Certainly when the holiday was over, she would make damned sure that she never found herself alone with him. Poor Eleanor. For a moment she felt quite sorry for her living with a slimeball such as Henry Nightingale, who wasn't half the man her husband was.

'What are you thinking about, sweetheart?' Alan asked when they were back in the hotel after the Venice trip, as she had been sitting at the mirror in their room for a long time staring at her reflection.

'Nothing.' She managed a smile. 'Nothing at all.'

*

Eleanor smiled a little wearily at the woman opposite. The restaurant was busy now and it was hardly an atmosphere conducive to discussing such a delicate matter as her daughter's concerns. If she were so much as to offer a crumb of criticism directed at Matthew, Paula would round on her. She felt sure of that for there was something of the tiger and the tiger cub about Paula.

'Paula ...' she began hesitantly. 'I'm not sure how to say this but Nicola's not very happy just now. She feels that Matthew is being a bit distant with her.'

'He's busy at work.'

'That's what I said. I said it would be work-related but she thinks not. She thinks it's something else.'

'It's not that Chrissie thing, is it? It's a while ago now. He told me all about that, about how they met accidentally and about how she rang Nicola to complain about him harassing her. The thing is, Eleanor, it doesn't surprise me in the least. I always knew that there was something a bit odd about Chrissie but I never let on. Why would I? You have to let these things run their course and nobody was more relieved than I was when she left. I could see what was coming.' She leaned forward, lowering her voice. 'I believe she was going to trap him, get pregnant and get him to marry her. I was worried sick that he would do the decent thing and that would have meant him giving up his place at university. I think he would have done it for her. But when she left, he took it hard. First love, that sort of thing ...' She looked towards Eleanor for some sort of understanding and Eleanor nodded. 'He's a deep thinker, is Matthew, and meeting her again just got to him, that's all. I thought it might. He's probably thinking about what might have happened if she hadn't moved away. Things like that don't last. They were still children and as soon as they go off to different universities to study that's it, isn't it? They meet other people and move on. Chrissie's gone now, married with children, so there's no need to worry and there's been no more contact so they should put it behind them now.'

'Are you sure there's been no more contact?'

'Yes, I am.'

'Nicola is suspicious. He's acting funny.'

'She's probably just imagining it, but that's between the two of them, isn't it? They are grown-ups, Eleanor, and we mustn't interfere.'

'Oh, come on, we can't just stand by and do nothing.'

'That's exactly what we must do.' Paula put her fork down. 'I wouldn't have liked it if my mother-in-law had butted in if something was up between me and Alan. Not that there ever was. We've been happy together. Alan's always been very loyal to me.'

The look was knowing and a little smug and Eleanor resented it. Did Paula know about Henry and his little dalliances over the years? Or did Paula imagine for one minute that her husband might be interested in her? She had caught a few glances between them during the holiday but that was just Henry playing at it. He couldn't help it. He would be trying to charm the ladies on his deathbed.

'We will see how things go,' Eleanor said. 'Whatever the problem is, it might blow over.'

'We will see and if there's any talking to be done to Matthew then I will do it,' Paula said, determination etched in her face. It left Eleanor feeling that it was Paula who was leading this conversation and that somehow during the course of this lunch there had been a distinct shift in their relationship. She had not anticipated any problems, for Paula was usually such a meek woman, anxious to please, maybe a little scared of her; but she was changed, her whole demeanour altered, and Eleanor did not care for it. It wrong-footed her and she had no idea how to deal with it. Should she tell her that Nicola was trying for a baby? She very nearly succumbed to that idea but Nicola had told her in confidence and all would be revealed in due course once she was pregnant. Although that might turn out to be a very bad idea if there was a problem with the marriage.

'We must keep in touch.' Eleanor knew she was not forgiven about the wretched dinner and determined that, should another invitation be forthcoming, she and Henry would be there like a shot.

'Yes we must and you and Henry must come along to dinner another time,' Paula said, giving in a little but refusing to look at the dessert menu as it was presented to them. 'I'm sorry but I'll have to cut this short because I have a meeting.'

'With whom?' She regretted the sharpness of the question for it was none of her business but Paula, who would previously have blushed at so direct a question, merely smiled.

'If you must know I'm meeting up with the agent who manages our rental properties. I have some ideas I want to discuss with him. I've had a look round them and they need considerable updating if we are to rent to a higher-end market.'

Eleanor stared at her. Where had she picked up that business-speak phrase? 'Oh, so you inherited properties as well? Isn't that lucky?'

'It's not lucky at all. It's family. And it's not just a few, it's practically a terrace. Alan's father was quite the entrepreneur.' Paula smiled at her and beyond the smile, Eleanor saw in her face that look of triumph. Paula Walker had blossomed and loved it. 'I hope that whatever happens in future you and I can keep in touch,' she went on. 'Although I'm sure that they will be just fine. Matthew adores her, you know. I don't know about Nicola. I never really know what she's thinking.'

'Trust me, she loves him very much too.'

'Well, then, we have nothing to worry about, do we?'

Out of habit Eleanor was just about to ask for the bill but Paula beat her to it, slipping her hand into the leather bag, an expensive number, and bringing out a credit card and adding a substantial cash tip.

My, my.

She was learning fast.

Chapter Seventeen

I T WAS NOT part of Nicola's brief to check through the rooms
at the hotel although, if a couple had booked the honeymoon suite, she did like to make sure that all was well there.
She unlocked the door and went inside, nodding with satisfaction because the first impression was that it looked good. She
smoothed down the quilt on the four-poster bed, fluffed up one
of the cushions, reflecting that she had never slept in a bed as
grand as this. She and Matthew had not come here for their
wedding reception, choosing another venue and also choosing
to forego the ubiquitous disco evening, opting to spend their
wedding night in an airport hotel prior to jetting off.

This room most certainly had that elusive wow factor, managing to be restful and romantic, with the curtains drawn back
to reveal the beauty of the gardens that were today bathed in
an autumnal low-lying mist, making them almost ethereal.

She was just checking the bathroom when the door opened
and one of the housekeeping staff came in. It was the girl with
the nose-stud and she looked startled as she saw Nicola.

'The room's been done,' Nicola said, nodding at her. 'Did
you do it?'

'Me and Connie.' The girl looked worried, chewing on her
lip.

'It looks good. Well done.'

'I couldn't remember if I'd done the end of the toilet roll, Mrs Walker,' the girl went on, flushed and flustered suddenly, tucking a blonde curl behind her ear. 'So I thought I would just check.'

'Thank you, it has been done and done very nicely. Tiffany, isn't it?'

'Yes, Mrs Walker.'

'How are you settling in?' She softened her voice.

It had come to her notice lately that her brusque attitude to lowlier members of staff had not escaped Gerry Gilbert's eagle eyes. He had spoken to her about it, at least she thought that was what he was referring to for he was the master of not quite saying what he was thinking. At any rate, he had called her into his office just after Val had been appointed to events manager, presumably to explain why she had not got the job. She was furious and had come very close to handing in her notice, but Matthew had told her not to do anything hastily and to stay cool and she was trying her damnedest to do that. She had even managed to offer smiling congratulations to Val when inside she was seething with indignation and jealousy. So the summons to Gerry Gilbert's office came as no surprise, for he had some explaining to do.

'You sent for me, Mr Gilbert?'

'Ah. Nicola. There you are. Take a pew. What do you think of Val?'

'She's very nice.' It was a pitiful response but the best she could come up with.

'Yes and she will fit in very well. She's a team player. She works well with everybody. She can adapt to both senior management and junior staff. It is important to remember that we are all part of the team. We are all in this together and often it's how the lowliest member of the team performs that matters.

Guests notice when the room maid smiles at them.'

Sitting opposite him at his desk, she listened as he then went off at a tangent, rambling on about running a tight ship but a happy ship and steering it through muddy waters into the calm of the harbour. In other words, one of his especially incomprehensible chats, but it made her think and as she watched the newcomer Val smiling her way through the corridors, dispensing happiness in her wake, she began to understand.

So there had to be a bit of a rethink about her own attitude and she was starting that right now with Tiffany.

'I'm doing all right.' Tiffany stood there awkwardly, duster in hand. 'Thanks for asking.'

Leaving her to her work, Nicola locked up the room and pocketed the key before taking the lift down to reception. She couldn't help smiling a little at the astonishment on the girl's face, for she may have expected a bollocking because, once the room was signed off, she should not be going back into it; toilet-roll end-pleating or no toilet-roll end-pleating. Being nice to minions was no bad thing. In fact, it made her feel rather good.

Now that Val was starting to make her mark on the way things were run, Nicola had to acknowledge, belatedly, that all in all she was doing a good job and that the changes she had made were beneficial. Also, to her surprise, she was finding that they were getting on rather well, which she would never have anticipated at the start.

Perhaps Gerry Gilbert knew what he was doing after all in appointing Val, whose CV did in fact read like a dream. Divorced, she was building a new life for herself and her teenage son here in the West Country and all credit to her for that. She was a chatty sort and had taken Nicola under her wing in more ways than one, a thing that a few months ago would have irritated the hell out of her.

Now she was a little more relaxed and simply taking it in her stride and yes, perhaps she did need a few more years' experience under her belt before she took on something more demanding.

The important thing now was to get her marriage back to where it had once been after the last few tricky months. That Chrissie business had made more of a mark on her than it should have and she struggled for a while believing her husband's account of it. Why had he gone to the station that day? There was still something a bit off about it all and she almost wished she could meet this woman and get it sorted out once and for all.

Suspicion and mistrust was an ugly thing and if she wasn't careful it would start to eat away at her and eventually destroy any trust she might have in Matthew. Her mother, despite the mess she had made of her own love life, was right about that. She had to let go of it. She had to trust Matthew as he trusted her.

But sometimes she did catch him staring into space with an expression she could not quite fathom and that was disturbing because on those occasions she always imagined that he was thinking about Chrissie. She recalled the woman's voice, pleasant-sounding even when she was not saying particularly nice things, and how she wished she had been more on the ball that day, but she was taken by surprise and when you are taken by surprise you can never think of the right things to say.

She might have a chat to Paula after all. She knew she had told her mother that they didn't get on, but she needed to know more about this Chrissie and Paula was the person who could tell her.

It was Paula's birthday soon, wasn't it, and that would be the perfect excuse for her to drop by the house and give her a present. She knew just the thing. And then, once she was inside and Paula had made them a cup of tea, she could weave the conversation round in a subtle way to the subject of Chrissie.

'Happy birthday! I know it is two days early but I was in town so I thought ...' Nicola stopped as Paula hugged her. It was a dutiful mother/daughter-in-law hug but it was less embarrassing than the formal greeting of a kiss on the cheek that could become so complicated with acquaintances. She had no idea what the form was these days. Was it one kiss on one cheek, a kiss on both cheeks or even three fleeting cheek kisses from one of her friends? When would it end? It was simpler when you shook hands or, in the old days, did a quick bob. She liked that idea, a quick bobbing up and down as in Jane Austen's day.

'It's lovely to see you, Nicola. What a surprise! It's all a bit messy. Come on in.'

If this was her idea of messy then God help her if she came to the cottage. She was increasingly aware that she was letting standards slip and the other day for some reason she had a blitz on it; got the Dyson out and cleaned it from top to bottom so that even Matthew noticed.

She handed over some flowers and the present, telling Paula that she wasn't to open it before her birthday so that there would be at least one surprise.

'Thank you. How exciting.' Paula took the present, a beautiful pashmina expertly wrapped by the lady in the shop, and put it aside. 'Alan always gets me perfume, which is very nice of course but hardly a surprise although, as you get older, you start to dread birthdays.'

She bustled off, searching for a vase for the flowers whilst Nicola waited in the lounge. There was some new furniture, she noticed, a new three-piece suite in cream leather – not to her taste – and a new television, one of those flat-screen things that just managed to stay the right side of good taste by not being too enormous.

She had worked it out on the way here what she was going to say, how she was going to gently get her to open up about Chrissie but in the event, as often happens, when confronted by the question in Paula's eyes that asked clearly why was she here, she just blurted it out.

'I thought that was all done and dusted,' Paula said, looking just a touch put-out. 'Matthew hasn't seen her again and he's not going to so it's best to forget it. Keep dragging it up will only cause a problem.'

'I know that but I'm just curious. Have you any other pictures of her other than the one I saw in your album?'

'I don't think so. That one just slipped through because, to be honest, I didn't like her. She was his first proper girlfriend and you know how intense it can get. I remember my first boyfriend. He was called Jack and—'

'I remember mine too,' Nicola put in swiftly before Paula got started. 'When you think back you wonder what the hell you saw in them, don't you?'

'Yes, I suppose you do. Anyway, Alan and I didn't want him to have a girlfriend because we were worried that it was going to affect his schoolwork because he was doing so well and on target for that Oxford place. It hadn't happened at that school before and he was under a lot of pressure to succeed. And we didn't want him to be too distracted with a girl, but it's very difficult to get the right balance between work and letting him have some fun and we didn't want to come over as heavy-handed because that never works.'

Nicola nodded, understanding completely and rather surprised that Paula had put it quite so succinctly.

'Why didn't you like her?'

'She was too clingy. She had not had a happy childhood and she was looking for another family. She pushed in. She was too sweet. She overdid it and it was creepy. Lucy didn't like her either and she was always a good judge of a person. She was not good for Matthew and I was concerned that she would not let him go, so it was a real relief when she moved away. Although he took it badly, he did buckle down to the work and he ended up getting that place. Lucy talked to him. He took a lot of notice of what his sister said.'

How would she have fared in the Lucy test? Would she have liked her? It was a sobering thought for she was not entirely convinced that Paula liked her either.

They changed the subject then, talking about shopping, and Paula took her upstairs to see the things she had bought. 'I had to have a personal shopper helping me,' she said a little shame-faced. 'So that I didn't keep making the same mistakes.'

'We all make mistakes. I would have helped you choose some new clothes,' Nicola told her, thinking that the personal shopper, whoever she might be, had come up with some surprising choices for such a tiny lady. 'We'll go shopping together some time.'

'I feel guilty at spending money,' Paula said when they were back downstairs. 'I can't get used to it. We've talked about it and we would like to give you and Matthew a little something if that's all right with you.'

'That would be lovely,' she said, thinking that a few hundred pounds would not come amiss to spend on the cottage or maybe put towards the holiday that they never seemed to get around to. And, if she did become pregnant, then it could go towards furnishing the nursery. She came close to telling Paula at that point that she was hoping to become pregnant soon, but what was the point until she actually was?

The rest of the visit was a touch forced as they ran out of things to say and there was no warmth in the goodbye hug accompanied with a murmured thank-you from Paula for the birthday present.

And for the first time, that coolness bothered her a good deal.

They had got off to a bad start and she realized only now how wrong she had been. But was it too late to make amends? Would the two of them ever be friends?

Chapter Eighteen

'IT'S ME. I'M back in Plymouth. On my own. Can we meet? I need to see you.'

His grip on the phone tightened and Matthew glanced round the office, but everybody was busy and nobody was remotely interested in his phone conversation. He turned his head slightly away, however, hoping that nobody was earwigging.

'How dare you ring me at work?' he said, voice low.

'Would you prefer that I ring you at home? I don't have your mobile number. If you remember, you chose not to give it to me.'

'I don't think we should meet,' he said, feeling the pressure as, across the room, somebody waved a hand at him, trying to attract his attention. 'I don't want you calling my wife again telling her that I'm harassing you when nothing is further from the truth. I don't want you to see you again, Chrissie. I tried to be polite because I didn't want to hurt your feelings but I really do not want to see you again.'

'I know that but I need to set a few things straight and this will be the last time. There is something very important that I need to tell you. I tried to tell you before but I couldn't bring myself to do it.'

'Damn you,' he muttered. 'But this had better be good.'

A time and place was agreed and he spent the rest of the morning thinking about it. He should have said no. Was he showing some weakness in agreeing to meet the woman who he was increasingly thinking was off her rocker? If this turned into a stalking situation proper then he would have to do something about it and he would leave her in no doubt this lunchtime about that. Her decision to ring Nicola had changed what had merely been a chance encounter with a face in the past, into something more important. By involving Nicola, Chrissie had upped the ante big time and he needed to get this sorted out once and for all.

She was supposedly a happily married woman or at the least she had been at pains to make it appear like that, and he was most definitely a happily married man. Nicola was being sweet to him these days when he knew he had been a bit off with her, worrying about this and that, some of it work-related because the big client was proving to be the most awkward guy he had ever dealt with. However she would not be so sweet with him if she found out that he was seeing Chrissie again so the first thing he needed to do was to ring her and tell her about this new development.

'I'm just about to meet some clients.' Nicola's voice was brisk. 'What's wrong?'

'Nothing's wrong,' he reassured her quickly. 'But Chrissie's rung me and asked me to meet for lunch. She says it's the last time but she has something desperately important to tell me.'

'She has a cheek. Do you want me to come with you? I could just about manage it if I set off after my meeting,' Nicola asked. 'That will make it wonderfully inappropriate won't it, if you turn up with me in tow?'

'It's not funny,' he told her. 'It's getting beyond a joke. I've never tried to contact her since she spoke to you and let her dare say I have.'

'Perhaps she needs closure,' Nicola said. 'Honestly, Matthew, just get it over with, but leave her in no doubt that this is the last time. Let her talk.'

'No danger of her not doing that.'

'Let her talk and then say goodbye and do tell her not to bother you again or this time it will be you accusing her of harassment. I think you have to be very firm about that. Poor besotted soul, she obviously can't take no for an answer.'

He felt marginally better that he had told Nicola and that she was taking it so well, but he felt some trepidation nonetheless as he made his way to the no-nonsense department-store café Chrissie had chosen as the venue. At least they could merge into the background here and after a brief nod of greeting – no hugs – they quickly got themselves a coffee and a couple of sandwiches before making their way to a corner table.

She looked very pale and very tired. She was wearing jeans, the same ones surely, tucked into high leather boots, and a silvery fur – faux fur he presumed – jacket. Her hair was faux red too, if there was such a term, and it didn't look good, dark roots showing, the style now looking just plain messy. She looked all of thirty-one, older even, and he felt bad for noticing, knowing how women hated to be reminded of the advancing years. She was too thin at that, her shape revealed as she shook off the jacket.

'How is your mother?' he asked politely, after they had extracted the sandwiches from their tricky packaging.

'She's not got long.' she said. 'It's spread to everywhere so it's just a matter of weeks. Days even. I've decided to stay until it's over.'

'I'm sorry to hear that. Is she in hospital?'

'No. She's back home being looked after by a Macmillan nurse. I've just popped out. I needed to get out.'

'I'm sorry,' he repeated. 'It must be hard for you.'

'It is. Marcus couldn't come with me because of his schedule and I didn't want the children to see their grandmother in
this state. They are being looked after,' she added as if worried
that he might think she had just abandoned them.

'They will be missing you.'

She nodded. 'It's very difficult. She's shrunk. She's just a
tiny lady now and she's had enough.'

'You just have to stay strong for her,' he said, feeling a little
helpless in this situation, understanding now why she looked
quite as rough as she did. He wanted to reach for her hand,
squeeze it, offer some sympathy but at the same time, he did
not want her to get the wrong end of the stick. Women were
so much better at this sympathy lark and he hoped to God she
was not going to break down in front of him. She looked in
control, but you never knew for sure.

'I wanted to meet face to face to apologize for what I did.
I should never have rung your wife. I don't know what came
over me. I'm sorry.'

'Nicola knows we're meeting today so there's nothing hole-
in-the-corner about this,' he told her.

'What did she say?'

'She feels sorry for you.'

'Why?'

He shrugged. They were not here to talk about his wife, his
very understanding wife, but it seemed that Chrissie was not
about to let it go.

'Was she very upset when I rang her?'

'What do you think?' he snapped, patience already wearing
thin. 'But she didn't take it too seriously when I explained.
She might have taken it seriously, though, if she hadn't been
so understanding, and it could have caused a big bust-up so it
wasn't a very bright thing for you to do, was it? Why did you
do it? You are happily married. It sounds as if you have a great
life with the kids and everything. You have no reason to feel

insecure surely?'

'Oh, Matthew, you have no idea. I would leave him tomorrow if I could. He's controlling. He's not violent, nothing like that, but he controls me emotionally,' she said. 'We fell out of love a long time ago, but the children ...' She sighed, putting down her slice of granary bread. 'It's not so easy when there are children, so I have to swallow my pride and stay.'

'I'm sorry,' he said, feeling genuinely sorry. 'And I'm sorry to keep saying that. Can you talk to anybody?'

'I'm talking to you, aren't I?' she said crisply. 'It brought it all to a head seeing you again. It made me realize that if my mum hadn't whisked me away then you and I would have got engaged and then married. We were a pair, Matthew, you and me. We were meant for each other. We would have been so very happy together.'

'I don't know about that,' he said, trying to laugh that one off. 'We were very young and I was about to go off to university. My mum reckons it would have faded away in any case.'

'What does she know about it?' The response was immediate. 'She never liked me, Matthew.'

'That's not true. My mother likes everybody. At least she always looks for the good side of everybody.'

'She did not like me. She thought I was too needy. She thought I was going to ruin your concentration. She once said as much in a roundabout way. But I think we would have found a way to be together, you and me. Didn't it mean anything to you at all?'

He was starting to feel uncomfortable as memories stirred. She was his first girlfriend, his first lover; his mother had thought it a platonic friendship but it had been more than that. Supposed to be studying, they slept together in his bedroom with the door unlocked and that had added to the excitement, for it meant somebody could walk in at any moment and that had bothered him more than it had Chrissie. His parents never had disturbed them because they respected his privacy, trusted him when he said that Chrissie was helping him with the studying, but Lucy had once caught them together and he had to swear her to silence.

'Lucy didn't like me either,' Chrissie said now, reminding him further. 'But then the feeling was mutual. Who did she think she was? Your keeper?'

'My sister,' he said, and suddenly it was too much. He guessed she had chosen this venue deliberately because it was not the place for an argument. 'And don't bring her into it.'

'I was sorry to hear about what happened to her,' she said. 'Bad luck.'

'Bad luck?' he echoed the words, aghast at the casual tone. 'It was the worst thing that has ever happened to me in my life.'

'Worse than me leaving you?'

'For God's sake, Chrissie, Lucy died. You can't compare it.' He paused, gathering himself together because he felt like leaving. 'Why are we here? What's the real reason? I'm not going to see you again, Chrissie. That would be one very bad idea.'

'I know. Don't worry, I'm not intending to harass you any more,' she said, the slightest of smiles – or was it a sneer? – covering her lips. She was wearing very pale pink lipstick and a lot of dark eye make-up, giving her a ghostly appearance. 'I just wanted to set the record straight.'

'And...?'

'I wanted you to know that I was pregnant when I left, pregnant with your baby.'

'What?'

'Why do you think we made such a quick move? It wasn't just about my mum and my stepdad, it was about me too. Mum acted like she was in some sort of Victorian melodrama when she found out. She could not bear the shame of her 16-year-old daughter having a baby, she said, and my stepdad had the chance of this job in Kent so it was an ideal opportunity. We moved away and nobody, none of Mum's friends, was any the wiser.'

'You were very nearly seventeen,' he said stupidly as if that made any difference, trying to take this in. A baby? He was a father already, then. 'What happened?' He was doing a quick calculation and fast coming to the conclusion that somewhere out there, there was a 14-year-old child belonging to him. 'Where is it? Did you have it adopted?'

'I lost it,' she said. 'So you needn't look so worried. I never had any intention of having it and I managed somehow to give myself an abortion. It's a wonder I didn't kill myself or make it impossible for me to have more children. I suppose I was lucky there.'

His heart settled back into a steady rhythm. 'Why are you bothering to tell me, then?'

'Because I can't keep it to myself any longer. I aborted your child and I think you ought to know, Matthew, that whatever it was between the two of us it was never just a teenage fling. It was much, much more for me. I've kept it secret from Marcus even though I sweated cobs when I did become pregnant in case there should be a problem, but there wasn't. Nicholas, as you no doubt saw at the station, is a healthy little boy and so is Victoria.'

'I'm sorry.' It seemed inadequate but he was sorry, thinking about her, about how desperate she must have been, about how she risked her life because of that desperation, and in the end it was all down to him. 'You should have told me,' he muttered as the shock dissipated. Around them, the sounds of the busy restaurant, the clatter of dishes, the scraping back of chairs, the chatter, grew less as the enormity of what she was telling him hit home.

'Why? What would you have done, Matthew?'

'I don't know,' he said. 'I honestly don't know. I expect I would have done the decent thing.'

She laughed. 'Oh, really. Are you telling me you would have given up your place at university for me?'

'We could have got round it,' he said, not sure how, though. 'I would have stood by you. I wouldn't have let you face it on your own.'

'You should see your face, Matthew Walker. And thank you, because I now know what I needed to know. You never loved me. Never. I would have gone to the ends of the earth for you but I doubt you would have gone further than Exeter for me.'

He sighed. What now? He couldn't make head or tail of this. What was she saying now? Why was she suddenly smiling?

'There was never a baby. Do you honestly think I was that naïve? I had all that business sorted out even at sixteen. But I just wanted to test you, to see your reaction.'

He remembered now that she was always good at lying. After making love, she would go down to the kitchen and brazen it out with his mother when he was having kittens thinking about it, hoping against hope that they had been quiet enough, that nobody had heard them. 'I've had enough of this.' He scrunched up the paper wrapping and left it on the tray, drained the last of his coffee. 'I'm off.'

'Goodbye.' She looked as if she was staying. 'Don't bother to wait for me. I'm going to have another coffee.'

He reached for his overcoat that was draped around the chair. 'How do I know what to believe any more? Are you really married to a pilot or is that a lie too? Do you have a house worth in excess of a million? Are those children yours?'

'Of course the children are mine, don't be ridiculous.'

'And the rest?' He held her gaze.

'Wouldn't you like to know?'

'And is your mother really dying, Chrissie? Or is that another little lie?'

'No, that happens to be true. But when it's over I am going and I am never coming back. Good luck, Matthew, but just remember one thing.'

He leaned down a little as she looked up at him and this time he saw the pain in her eyes, helpless because there was nothing he could do to help, but he had to harden his heart to it because he had no other choice.

'I love you. Goodbye Matthew.' She mouthed the words, a blush staining her pale cheeks, and he just nodded, managing a tight smile before walking away. His mind was in a whirl. He had no idea how much of all that was true, whether the talk of a baby was really just a mischievous test or not. The fact was, if it was just a test for him, a very bitter sort of test, when she had talked about a pregnancy, about an abortion, she had just delivered an Oscar-winning performance.

He knew he had promised himself that there would be no more secrets between him and Nicola, but this time he would make an exception to that. He hoped that he might persuade his wife to put aside her very real fears and have a baby, but it would have to be her decision and he wasn't going to put undue pressure on her.

If he was not meant to be a father then so be it. If Chrissie had had a baby then perhaps it had been adopted. Maybe there was a 14-year-old boy or girl – his child – living somewhere with someone else and he would never ever see it.

Chrissie had engineered this last meeting quite deliberately. She had planted that thought in his head – is it true or isn't it? – just to make sure that he would never forget her.

But for his peace of mind he had to do just that.

Chapter Nineteen

Autumn was tumbling fast into winter, the days had shortened, storms had lashed the area, causing floods and severe wind damage, but mercifully their cottage and the trees along the banks of the river had escaped most of it.

And Nicola was pregnant.

Just. She had not yet told Matthew because she wanted to be a little further on before she did so. So far she had managed to contain the throwing-up to times when he was not around but it had not worked so well at work and Barbara had guessed – rightly this time – and offered her congratulations, although she was sworn to silence as yet. Damn it, she never meant to tell the woman before she told her husband but she could hardly deny it when she asked outright and she was being very considerate, bringing her a packet of ginger biscuits next day: Barbara's remedy for morning sickness.

She would tell Gerry Gilbert in due time and of course it would be no surprise whatsoever to him for hadn't he been willing a pregnancy on her for ages now? She could not keep the secret much longer from her mother, who was eyeing her up closely whenever she saw her, but Matthew should be the first to know.

How could she have ever thought that she did not want

children? She was amazed at how quick the turnaround had been. Already, with the baby the size of a bean, she was feeling protective towards it and with Matthew getting people in to work on the cottage things were looking up. She had finally admitted to herself that she had been behaving like a spoilt child, wanting to run before she could walk.

Matthew was right. She had to remember how she felt when she first set eyes on this cottage. It was not as bad as all that, for after all, hadn't she fallen in love with it back then? She had to return to that feeling and start thinking of it again as the sweetest little cottage imaginable. They just needed to get through the winter and keep warm and when spring came they would be fine for a while longer and the spare room would make an adequate nursery when baby arrived in summer.

She was mellowing and becoming more like Paula every day. It was very worrying. She was nest-building already and she was barely properly pregnant yet. What on earth would she be like by the end of it when she was the size of an elephant?

Rare for her, she had a Saturday free and it promised to be a lazy day for both of them but, to her surprise, after breakfast – the smell of Matthew's bacon sandwich nearly made her throw up – he suggested they take a trip out.

'Where?' She could not hide her astonishment for, on his day off, he was usually perfectly happy to lounge around doing nothing.

'Just out. It's lovely out there, we don't want to be cooped in all day long.'

'It's cold out there,' she said, thinking that for once it felt much cosier indoors. Despite her complaints, it was proving warmer here than she had first thought, the thick walls keeping the heat in; a huge pile of logs had just been delivered and, to top it all, she had finally got the hang of lighting the fire.

'Wrap up, then,' he said, determined, it would seem, to get her out and about. 'Come on and we'll stop off for lunch later.'

'Where are we going?' she asked but infuriatingly he would not say, setting off across the bridge and passing the 'Welcome to Devon' sign. Feeling a little grumbly because she had got ready far too quickly and was feeling a touch nauseous already, she had to admit that it was a glorious late-autumn day, the trees slow to lose their leaves and outdoing each other with the blaze of oranges, yellows, and reddish browns.

Already her mother was talking about Christmas plans, something she liked to organize well in advance, and it was arranged that she and Matthew would be going to them on Christmas Day and to Paula and Alan's on Boxing Day. That suited her fine as she was never absolutely sure whether or not she might be called in to work, as the Christmas schedule was always subject to sudden change. Being readily available when required was a prerequisite for future promotion although, as of now, with maternity leave looming, that was becoming an ever-fainter possibility.

And just now she could not care less.

'I don't fancy a long walk if that's what you have in mind,' she said, noting that they were approaching walking country. 'I hate surprises. You should know by now that whenever you surprise me I'm always wearing the wrong things. Look at my boots. They are not made for walking.'

He laughed. 'Don't worry. There's no serious walking involved.'

'I hope you've not booked lunch at somewhere too posh,' she went on, getting more irritated by his obvious amusement. 'Because I would never have worn this jacket if I'd known.'

Matthew slowed, indicated and turned right and she realized that they were going towards the village, the village where she had dragged him a couple of times to view Tall Trees. For God's sake, she did not want to be reminded of it, not when she

187

was finally getting her head round living at the cottage.

They drove through the village and he drew to a halt, switched off the engine.

The For Sale board was still there, propped up beside the imposing gateway but this time there was something laid across it: an Under Offer sticker. Well, thanks a million for that. It would be some sodding London couple buying it as a second home, donning their country wellies a few weeks a year when they deigned to put in an appearance.

'What have you brought me here for?' She could not help the exasperation in her voice. 'You know damned well we can't afford it. You sat me down and talked me through the figures.'

'It's ours, darling,' Matthew said. 'We complete very soon. I made a very low offer but they accepted, delighted to have a sale at last and a cash one at that. I can't have the keys yet but the agent is meeting us in a few minutes and she's happy for us to have a look round without her. They've moved all the furniture out, by the way, so it's not going to look quite the same as it did the first time we viewed it.'

'But ...' she stepped out of the car and stood a moment gazing at it, the house she had dreamed of so often, the house they could not afford. It stood, an higgledy-piggledy stone-built house in grounds that wrapped round the property, and she could rhyme off the details in her head: square hall, sitting room with bay window, dining room across the hall, a large kitchen, study/music room, snug, conservatory, five bedrooms, three bathrooms. All this with a separate annexe in the former stable block that she had earmarked as having great potential for something or other.

Wow.

The agent was waiting for them by the entrance, her car parked round the back. She greeted them, all smiles, and handed them the keys, saying she would hang around until they were ready.

Matthew opened the door and she followed him into the echoey space. The previous owners were gone and it was empty, their footsteps loud on the tiles of the hall. It looked different without the rugs and the pictures and the ornate mirror but the red carpet on the stairs was still there and they had left the glamorous if slightly incongruous modern chandelier that was either a pièce de résistance or a disaster. She would have to reserve judgement on that.

'I know,' Matthew said, following her gaze. 'Horrendous, isn't it?'

'Matthew, what on earth are you doing? How much did you offer? How can we afford it?' she said, commonsense taking over. 'We did the sums and we decided we couldn't. And we haven't sold the cottage either. And what's this about a cash sale?'

'Mum's given us some money so we can do this,' he told her. 'I've gone through the sums and it's OK. And I think she might have half an eye to her and Dad moving into the annexe one day. It will make a great self-contained granny flat and I can draw up the plans for that in no time. It's already got the green light so there won't be a problem.'

'Wait a minute. You mean they might want to move in with us?'

'Maybe. Someday. She's had second thoughts about moving just at the moment. She likes her house. I know that might surprise you but she does. And Dad's in no hurry to give up the business and it's better for him to be living in the city to do that. The bulk of his business comes from students.'

The thought of Paula and Alan living in the annexe was not ideal but Nicola concentrated on the words 'maybe' and 'someday'. She could live with that thought, for it was so far into the future it hardly counted. Paula and Alan were hardly in their dotage, not yet.

'She's been very generous,' she said as the enormity of what

Paula had done started to sink in. She had thought Paula meant a few hundred not several thousand. 'She said something last time I saw her about giving us something but I didn't think you would be too keen on that.'

'I wasn't at first but she was very persuasive. What's the point, she said, of you being left a load of money when we die when you need it now? You're right, I would much rather do this ourselves but it's going to be a very long time before we can afford to buy something like this and so we have to be realistic.'

'You mean you have to swallow your pride,' she said with a small smile. 'Thanks for that, Matthew.'

'Thank my mum. She's really happy to do it.'

'What about your father? You haven't mentioned him.'

'It was Mum's idea that we have the money but he's fine too. He wants us to have this house. He knows what it means to you and he told me that we should keep the ladies happy if we can.'

'It's still a lot of money and we shouldn't take it from them.' She was weaving her way through the rooms, decorating them already in her head. Five bedrooms were more than they needed but they could do them one at a time. Now that the dream was coming true, she was oddly more hesitant than Matthew. 'Is Paula sure about this?'

'Absolutely. She insists and have you noticed she's got very bossy lately? I've been thinking about it and we can put the cottage up for sale again but rent it in the meantime.'

'And we can be in here by Christmas. We can have Christmas here,' she said, excitement taking over. 'We can put the tree over there by the window and we can invite everybody here and I can cook a lovely Christmas lunch, if I'm not working, that is.'

'Don't get carried away. And we don't do that much at Christmas, not my family. It's not a good time for us so we don't really celebrate.'

'I know and I know why, but I think it's time you did. We can try to make it as happy as we can. I know it was her birthday but Lucy wouldn't have wanted you to be miserable, not at Christmas.'

'You are right.' He was just standing there, looking at her, delighted at her reaction as, unable to stop herself, she gave a little jig of excitement, her eyes shining.

A moment later, she flew over to him, her face buried a moment in his shoulder. 'This is the best surprise ever. And by the way ...' Daft time to say it, but she could not wait a minute longer. 'I'm pregnant.'

'I thought so.' He hugged her to him. 'I wondered when you would get round to admitting it.'

Nicola had never met the old man, her grandfather-in-law, who had been indirectly responsible for giving her the house of her dreams and now, when it was too late, she wished she had met him because who knows, she, an outsider, might have gone some way towards sorting out their ridiculous feud. She knew they all felt guilty about taking Thomas Walker's hard-earned money, but it was family money and it was their due.

Anyway, like Matthew, she had accepted Paula's kind offer with as much humility as she could muster, visiting her and bringing her a big bunch of red roses as a small thank-you.

'Come on in,' Paula said, seeming genuinely pleased to see her, sniffing the roses and saying that she shouldn't have. 'Come in and sit down and I'll put the kettle on. How are you, Nicola? Matthew tells me you are pregnant. Congratulations. We are very excited and your mother must be thrilled.'

'She is. How are you, Paula? How are the driving lessons going?'

'Very well. I'm a natural, the instructor says, although maybe he says that to everybody. I was a bit nervous at first.'

'Of course you were. We are all nervous when we start

lessons. What does Alan say about it?'

'To tell the truth, he wasn't keen on the idea. He says the roads are too busy and he says that even if I pass I'll have to have extra lessons before he lets me loose on the motorway.'

'Ignore him,' Nicola said. 'I'm a much better driver than Matthew and you'll be absolutely fine. I'm surprised at Alan. You would think he would be delighted that you're finally taking the plunge.'

'Well, he isn't. I think he'd be delighted if I failed.'

'Don't be daft.' Nicola saw the doubt in her eyes, though, and wondered just what was the matter with Alan. Surely he liked his new improved wife? However, she thought it wise not to pursue it further.

'Are you missing work, Paula?'

'No. Well, perhaps a bit, but the thing is I was offered a promotion before I left,' she went on, looking around as if somebody was eavesdropping. 'I had just made up my mind not to take it and was worried about how I would tell them so it was a relief when we got the money because then I could tell them to stuff the job. Well, not quite that, but it was a wonderful reason to leave.'

Nicola laughed. She had never heard Paula say anything remotely like that in all the time she had known her. But then, as her mother had said, having money had changed her. And definitely for the better. She had a sparkly look about her and it was nothing to do with the neat fitted dress she was wearing. She didn't have it quite right, not yet, for the colour did her no favours, but she was getting there in the style stakes.

'I don't miss the card shop but I'm much too young to retire,' she went on. 'I need to take up a hobby of some kind before I start getting bored.'

'Why don't you? It's a marvellous opportunity to do something you've always wanted to do. Travel. Learn Chinese. Start piano lessons.'

'I don't know about the travelling but I might take up quilting,' Paula said thoughtfully and, exchanging a glance, they both laughed.

'Don't be too adventurous,' Nicola warned her, still smiling. She was warming to Paula more and more. There was more to her mother-in-law than first thought and she was reminded that first impressions of people should always be taken with a pinch of salt.

'Don't laugh but I'm thinking of joining the local Amateur Dramatic Society,' Paula said as they sat companionably enough in silence for a while.

'Good heavens, are you? I didn't know you were interested in acting.'

'It's not something I usually admit.' And then, a little shyly, Paula told her about the acting, how she would have loved to be on stage, and hearing that, seeing the sparkle in her eyes as she talked about it, pulled at Nicola's heart because the poor woman, just like Alan, had never been given the encouragement they needed from their parents. It made her realize that she would give her child – a slightly larger bean now – every opportunity and never ever stand in its way. If it wanted to go to Mars, she would be the first to push it onto that spaceship.

'What do you think?' Paula asked. 'Should I try?'

'Go for it. I shall drag you there if necessary.' She leaned forward, thinking that today was the first time ever they had really clicked. 'I didn't know the old man, Matthew's grandfather,' she told her. 'But Matthew told me something about him and he was wrong, you know. Alan couldn't have done better than you if he tried.'

She had no idea why she said it, why she dared to voice it out loud but she did.

And, when she eventually left, for the first time ever, the hug they exchanged on the doorstep was truly meant.

Chapter Twenty

'PAULA, I NEED to see you. It's Eleanor. Can we meet somewhere?'

Paula was in the middle of tearing up the particulars of the various houses the estate agent had sent them. The houses were in different areas of the city but, although they had viewed a lot of them, she had never really fancied any of them. Her heart had never been in a move, not just now, and although there was some confusion – for a while she was going to go through with it because she thought that was what Alan wanted – it eventually became clear that he had no particular desire to move either.

She knew they could be accused of being stick-in-the-muds but they liked it here so why should they move? It was a street of well-kept houses with good neighbours, which was worth a lot because you could never be sure who you got landed with next door. They could spend money now on a new bathroom, something really nice, and she was not fussed about a big garden either. The big pots in the back courtyard here were good enough for her.

And, although she and Alan had no intention of ever moving into the 'granny flat' at Matthew and Nicola's new house, she had to say that in order for her stubborn son to accept the money she offered him.

So she was tearing up and stuffing the particulars into the bin bag when the phone rang and picking it up, she never expected it to be Eleanor because Eleanor never did ring. And she sounded different, panicky, anxiety etched into the voice.

'Where are you?' she asked, tempted to ask her to calm down because she sounded distraught.

'I'm in town. I'm parked in Drake Circus. Do you want to meet somewhere for lunch?'

'Look ...' She had the fire lit, it was cold outside and the thought of getting herself into town through an already murky gloom was not an attractive one. 'Why don't you come to me? I can do us a quick lunch. Would some soup and a sandwich be all right? The soup won't be home-made, I'm afraid.'

'It would be marvellous. I can be with you shortly. Are you sure it's all right? I don't want to impose on you.'

'You won't be. Come on round. I'll have the kettle on.'

Eleanor was wearing a pale-grey cashmere coat, long and loose, over trousers and sweater. She looked tired but her hair was sleek and pulled back, her make-up as clever and subtle as always.

'This is so good of you, Paula,' she said, taking off her gloves and handing Paula the coat and the toning scarf in the manner of a lady to her maid. Everything always matched, Paula thought, knowing that, even with her increased spending power, she still struggled to achieve the best look for herself.

'I felt so rotten suddenly that I didn't know what to do. I shouldn't have come in today but I had an appointment with one of our team and I couldn't put it off. We've had a hiccup with something and that husband of mine has been trying to keep it from me because he didn't want to worry me.'

'I'm sorry. Is it serious?'

'Nothing that can't be sorted but I do wish he wouldn't keep things from me. We are supposed to be equal partners but if anything does go wrong it's always me who picks up the pieces.'

'Come on through and we'll have a cup of tea first. Unless you prefer coffee?' she asked, showing Eleanor into the lounge. 'Go and sit by the fire.'

'A real fire. How wonderful.' She saw Eleanor looking round before she made a positive little comment about how nice the room looked. She had no idea whether she was speaking the truth, but she no longer minded so much. Eleanor could make of it what she would and it did not compare in any shape or form with the splendour of her house but it was Paula's home and she loved it. And just lately she had realized how much she loved it when she had considered leaving it.

'Sorry, I should have brought you some flowers,' Eleanor said, sitting down in Alan's chair by the fire. They had a coal fire these days, ever since they had gone to the trouble of having the chimney sorted out, and it was lovely and warm in the room, a proper winter's day outside, the temperature dropping sharply this last week. 'I just haven't been able to think properly these last few days.'

'I won't be a minute.'

Paula bustled about in the kitchen, eventually bringing in the tea. 'Isn't it wonderful news about the baby,' she said, making room for the tray on a small table. 'And Nicola seems to be keeping well.'

'She is. The sickness isn't quite so bad now. She's scared stiff about having it but we can help there, can't we? We can reassure her. I blame all these television programmes about midwifery and showing people giving birth. It's enough to put anybody off. Did you have an easy time with yours?'

'Fairly.' Paula smiled. This was the sort of conversation she could handle with one hand tied behind her back. Female and gossipy. She settled back comfortably in her chair. She was wearing ballerina pumps which made her feel so tiny; but it was her home, her space, and it no longer mattered that Eleanor was almost a foot taller. 'Matthew was straightforward but Lucy was premature and small and we were worried for her because her lungs were weak – but she was a little fighter.'

Eleanor smiled sympathetically, sipping her tea.

Paula hesitated. 'I don't usually talk about it,' she began. 'It's too painful but it's getting better and I feel badly about that because it's as if I've got over it and I haven't and I never will. Not completely. But I do forget about it sometimes, find myself laughing, and for a long time that seemed a sort of betrayal to Lucy.'

'I'm sure that's a very natural reaction. And I'm sorry I tried to push you into talking about it. I should know by now, from my limited experience, that people only do that in their own time.'

'You never think it's going to happen to you,' Paula said, not quite sure why she suddenly felt the need to talk. Perhaps she was giving Eleanor some time because she knew that there was something wrong and that she was plucking up courage to come out with it. 'She had a sore throat and I thought it was the start of flu or something like that. Anyway, I phoned the school to say she wasn't coming in and then I left her in bed and went off to work. I didn't work at the card shop then but at a baker's just down the road so I told her I would pop back at lunchtime and check how she was and she was to ring me if she felt bad. I left the handset beside the bed and a jug of water and a few biscuits and I told her to stay put and to ignore the doorbell if anybody rang it. I did all the things I normally did. It wasn't the first time I'd left her on her own for a few hours.'

'That sounds perfectly reasonable. She was thirteen, old enough to be left.'

'Oh yes,' Paula said quickly. 'She was very responsible. A

good girl. But by the time I got home at lunchtime she was struggling to breathe and that had never happened before. She had tried to ring me but couldn't manage it and that scared me. I managed to get hold of Alan eventually – he always left phone numbers for his clients with me in case I ever ...' She tailed off. 'Anyway, he told me to ring for an ambulance straightaway. When they came ...' She paused, re-living the moment. 'The man said that I wasn't to worry, that the pain she was feeling was most likely because she had pulled a muscle in her chest from coughing and that she should probably just stay in bed and rest and it would get better. But when his colleague came up, he looked more worried and we set off for the hospital and then halfway there the blue lights came on and I knew then it was serious. And when we got there, she was whisked into intensive care straightaway and hooked up to machines before you knew it. There were all these machines, blinking ...' she made a little sound and put her hand over her mouth.

'What was it?'

'She was shutting down. The doctor explained it to me later. It was like lights going out in a house, one room at a time, until they were all off and it was complete darkness. It was called sepsis.'

Eleanor nodded. 'I've heard of that but I didn't know it was as serious as that.'

'It can be very quick. The body goes into shock followed by multiple organ failure and then that's it. If it reaches a certain stage there is nothing they can do.'

'Oh, Paula, what can I say?'

'It's all right.' She managed a smile. 'But if I hadn't gone to work that day, if I had got her to hospital earlier, then she would have stood a chance. Half an hour might have made a difference. But I didn't. I delayed it because I rang Alan first when I should have rung for the ambulance. But you don't like to bother them, do you, not when you're not sure what it is. You don't want to be a nuisance.' She looked across at Eleanor. 'You would have done it differently, wouldn't you, if it had been Nicola? You would have got her to that hospital and played merry hell until somebody did something, wouldn't you? Oh I wish I was more like you, Eleanor, then I might have saved her. If I hadn't been such a wimp, frightened of bothering people, then I might have saved my little girl.'

'Oh, don't say that.' Eleanor was across the room in an instant, sitting beside her on the sofa and putting her arms round her. She smelled of a lovely scent and Paula closed her eyes a moment, taking it in, taking in the comfort she was offering, composing herself to stop a flood of tears. She was past crying about Lucy and here it was, welling up as if it were yesterday.

'If Lucy was here today she would not blame you,' Eleanor was saying in a calm, quiet voice. 'She loved you and you were so lucky to have such a loving relationship with her. I want you to hold onto that thought. I've never quite had that with Nicola. She's always been a touch abrasive, never one for a cuddle; or is that me perhaps? It's only recently that it's starting to get better now that she's pregnant. She's changed a bit and I'm happier because I think the two of them will be fine. They seem a lot happier these days.'

'The three of them,' Paula corrected her, moving away and sniffing away the tears. 'Thanks. And you were right. It has helped to talk about it. I've kept it shut up for too long. I've never really talked about it with anybody, not even Alan. You know, the first thing he said to me when they brought us the news in hospital was that it wasn't my fault and because he said that, in my eyes that made it absolutely one hundred per cent my fault.'

'How did you make that out?'

'I don't know. Grief comes at you like that. Blaming myself

was my way of coping with it. And it's only now, all these years later, that I can stop doing it because it's not helping is it? Oh dear …' She pulled herself together. 'I'll put the soup on. And I've made a selection of sandwiches and then maybe you can tell me what's wrong with you.'

Paula had set things out in the dining room, a small room off the kitchen, but then everything about this house was small. Goodness, Eleanor reflected that she could fit the entire house into her sitting room – well, almost.

But what did it matter? What did things matter? After what Paula had told her, after what seemed a distinct warming in their relationship, she found something comforting in the little dining room where white dishes were laid on the blue table-cloth. There was vegetable soup and big chunks of bread, a little dish with butter, and a plate piled with sandwiches with the crusts trimmed. And a big pot of tea, a little matching sugar bowl and milk jug.

She had no appetite but she did her best to do it justice and then Paula brought out some cheese and grapes and they sat together and finally, as if it were after a long period of sniff-ing around each other suspiciously, it seemed as if they were friends.

'I want to thank you,' Eleanor told her. 'For helping the youngsters out with the house. It was very kind of you and a real boost for them to be able to move from the cottage. We would have helped of course except that I'm not sure if we could have helped to the extent you did. Our money is rather tied up at the moment.'

'You're not in trouble, are you? We can help if you need it.'

'Thank you, that's very sweet of you but no, it happens occa-sionally and we've always got through it. Henry is a wheeler and dealer. Sometimes I have to close my eyes to the things he gets up to. Between you and me, some of it is a little too under the counter if you know what I mean?'

Paula nodded, not the least surprised by that. Crooks come in all shapes and sizes. 'If you do need help just say and I am so pleased we could help Matthew and Nicola. After all, what use is it to have a big amount of money just hanging around? We've invested some of it for the future and we still have the rents coming in from the houses so we are fine and it seemed only right that we helped them out before the baby comes.'

'Nicola is very excited about it all. She has big plans and I've said she can help herself to some of the bigger items we have stored away for clients. It's going to take a lot of furniture to fill those rooms.'

'How is Henry?'

The question was guarded and Eleanor glanced quickly at her. 'He's all right. You know Henry.'

'Yes, I think I do.'

It was just something in the way she said it, something that told Eleanor that she knew all there was to know about Henry. So what was the use of denying it?

'We have an unconventional marriage. It's not quite the same as yours,' she explained. 'I think you've probably guessed that he's a bit of a free spirit.'

'You mean he's unfaithful?'

She looked at her in surprise. She had meant that but she had not expected Paula to be quite as direct. Somehow she thought of Paula as being innocent but maybe she was not as innocent as she appeared.

'He didn't try it on with you, did he?'

Paula shrugged. 'A little but I guessed as much anyway. When we were on holiday I think the whole group of us had him down as a ladies' man. He's very attractive and he's touchy-feely if you know what I mean.'

'I know exactly what you mean.'

Having finished their meal, Paula put down the napkin

and suggested they return to the living room and no, she did not need any help because she would pop the dishes in the machine later, thanks very much. 'Oh, you have a dishwasher,' Eleanor said in a voice that implied surprise as if she had expected Paula to be putting on the rubber gloves at the sink.

'Yes, we have a dishwasher,' she said with a smile. 'In fact Alan says I have more gadgets now in my kitchen than the shuttle control room at Houston.'

Eleanor waited to resume the conversation once they were settled in front of the newly banked-up fire. 'I thought I didn't mind,' she went on as, opposite her, Paula sat quietly, her turn now to listen and sympathize. 'But it was when I was talking to Nicola a while ago, that I realized that I did mind. And I mind particularly that she knew about it as she grew older. I should have had the courage to leave him a long time ago, but it was difficult to make that decision. It's always much easier to stay put and I thought it might get better, but it never did. He just can't keep his hands to himself and it is too late now for him to change.'

'Then leave him. Why don't you?'

'We run the business together so it's not as simple as that and it's up to me to try to keep him on the straight and narrow. And there's that "better the devil you know" thing as well. I'm used to it by now. I shouldn't let it upset me. Tell me, Paula, what it was he did to you on holiday? I must know.'

Her face pink with embarrassment, Paula told her and Eleanor listened, her face growing grim.

'I'm so sorry. I can't believe he did that. Well, I can believe it but to do it there in that café is almost beyond belief. He is so arrogant. He's having a fling with somebody at this very moment. She's divorced, a rich widow, in her forties, no children, very smart.'

'You know her, then?'

'I don't know her but I know what she looks like. I don't

know where they meet or how often but I just know when he's been with her. And the laugh is, he still thinks I haven't a clue. How arrogant is that?'

'I'm so sorry. What are you going to do?'

'As usual, nothing. I haven't got the fight in me just now, not with the way things are.'

'There's something else, then?'

'Yes.' She hesitated because once it was said it made it real. 'I'm not well. I have an appointment sometime next week at the hospital and I want you to come with me, Paula. Please say you will. I don't want to worry Nicola and there's nobody else I can ask.'

'What about Henry?'

Eleanor gave her a look. 'After what we've just talked about, he is the last person I want with me. You will come, won't you?'

'Of course I will.'

Chapter Twenty-One

Eleanor did not allow her standards to slip even for the hospital appointment.

She was wearing the grey coat with black high-heeled boots and a black furry hat under which her hair managed to remain unruffled.

December had arrived and with it the first snow flurries. They did not often get snow, not in this part of the world, but as they hurried into the hospital from the car park, it was starting to stick to the pavement, the flakes heavier by the minute.

'I'm afraid there's a bit of a wait,' the receptionist told them when they had made their way to the required department. 'Dr Gibson has been delayed but she will get to you as soon as possible.'

'It's a woman doctor, then,' Paula muttered as they took a seat amongst other worried-looking ladies. 'That's good, isn't it?'

'It doesn't matter to me. I have no preferences. It could be a monkey as far as I'm concerned so long as it knows its job. I could have gone private, Paula, but somehow I felt on this occasion that—'

'You don't have to explain,' Paula said, nervous herself now as she caught a pleading look in the eye of a nearby woman.

She sensed the whole room was bristling with anxiety, women screaming inside but trying, as women do, to stay focused by leafing through the many cheap and cheerful magazines lying around. Today though, she did not feel she would be cheered up in any way by reading about the antics of minor celebrities and she was not a patient. 'It's just the waiting that's going to be hard, but you will know the result by lunchtime. We can have a lovely lunch somewhere afterwards. My treat.'

'I'll take you up on it but only if I don't have cancer,' Eleanor said in a matter-of-fact tone. 'If I have, then the last thing I will want is a slap-up lunch. In fact, I'm not sure how I will cope with it. I'm not a woman who can cope, never have been. I need to be fit and well. I always have been and I don't do illness.'

'If the worst happens, it won't be the end of the world, but let's be positive. I know loads of women who've found a lump and it's been just a cyst. Alice next door to me used to get them regularly. She used to have to go and have them drained. She said it used to be such a relief when they stuck a needle in and the liquid drained out. And didn't the doctor tell you it was probably just a cyst because it was moving around and that you weren't to worry?'

'For God's sake, Paula, shut up.' To soften the words, Eleanor reached over and took her hand, and Paula gave it a little squeeze. She understood something of what she was going through but she was working on the theory that keeping talking, however much nonsense, would take her mind off it a bit.

'Eleanor Nightingale!' A nurse with a clipboard appeared and Eleanor nearly fell over the chair as she stood up, discarding the coat and going across. Trying to stop the beautiful material from sliding onto the floor, Paula just had time to say 'Good luck'.

She was back shortly.

'I've had another mammogram,' she said, resuming her

seat. 'And then I'll be called for an ultrasound. Isn't that when they put the jelly on you?'

'I think so. And then what?'

'Then the doctor will see me to discuss the results. Will you come in with me?'

'Of course I will. If that's what you want.'

'Thanks, Paula.' She was not far away from tears and it was so unlike Eleanor that it left Paula struggling to come up with a positive. Poor Eleanor, not only was she having to cope with Henry but here she was in danger of having to cope with a serious illness. If it was her who had found the lump in her breast then she knew who would be beside her at this moment.

Alan.

She was left on her own again when Eleanor went for the scan a little later and then they were left waiting once more. A few people came and went; one lady having to be helped away by her friend, so presumably it wasn't good news for her.

'Oh, God,' Eleanor had murmured at that point. 'That might be me, Paula. I'm hopeless with bad news. I shall be a wreck.'

'No you won't. You might be surprised at your reaction. You forget that I've been through the worst thing that can ever happen to a mother.' She was sorry to bring it up but she needed Eleanor to stop being so pathetic and tough talking was the answer. 'You deal with it. You have to. There's no alternative and if it is bad news then you have to take what you can from it. Be positive. There is treatment to be had,' she said, scratching round for good facts. 'It's no longer the death sentence it might have been once upon a time. Women live for years with it. They get on with their lives and you can do the same. And remember, you are not on your own. You have Nicola and you have me and before long we'll have a grand-child to spoil.'

That was quite a speech and she had surprised even herself. If Eleanor heard it she made no comment, simply picking up a magazine and turning the pages. On the wall, the clock ticked steadily round. People still came and went. This was like waiting for an execution and they had started to run out of things to say. Talking trivia was not going to work, not now, for even an attempt to talk about possible names for their expected grandchild had met with a muted response. Apparently Nicola had decided on them. Clementine if it was a girl and Daniel if it was a boy.

'Do you want a drink?' Paula looked round, spotting a cabinet nearby. 'There are some drinks and bars of chocolate. Shall I get us something?'

Eleanor, past words now, simply shrugged and Paula, rifling in her bag for loose change, set off. It was something to do even though she did not particularly want a drink, but it was better than staring at the walls and at the reception desk. And then, after waiting what seemed hours – what *was* hours – just as she was putting the coins in the slot, Eleanor's name was called. A young female doctor wearing a white coat over a dark suit was standing there with a smile on her face.

Was there significance in the smile?

Jolting to her feet, Eleanor looked round for her and Paula, giving up on the drinks at once, hurried to her side.

Chapter Twenty-Two

'LET ME GET this straight. Are you telling me we're destitute, Henry?'

'No. Hell, no. I've just lost a fair bit of money, that's all. I've had to pay everybody back with interest just to keep them quiet. I honestly believed those paintings were genuine. Derek's been leading me up the garden path for years. I've never trusted him.'

'I never trusted him, you mean.' Eleanor said. 'And if you hadn't been so greedy it wouldn't be so bad. You shouldn't have taken on so many of them expecting a huge return and now they are worth almost nothing. It was a close thing, Henry, this time. You could have ended up in jail. They are forgeries, aren't they?'

'Not to my knowledge,' he said, looking shifty as hell.

'You're not being questioned under oath,' she told him. 'So you might as well be honest with me.'

'I am being honest. How on earth was I supposed to know they were a bit iffy? As far as I was concerned they were the genuine article attributed to that bloody awful Scottish artist. How delighted were we to find a load more pictures after he topped himself, especially when there were people falling over themselves to own one? I bought them off Derek, sold them on and as far as I was concerned it was all strictly above board. Anyway, I don't trust half of these so-called art experts. Who are they to say that they aren't the genuine article?'

'Don't push it, Henry, or you will make things worse. You were more than happy to put your trust in Derek and it's backfired.'

'That's right. Make me out to be some sort of crook. You've turned a blind eye to it for years, darling, so don't come the angel with me, not now. Anyway, it's sorted, the panic is over and we're only a few thousand adrift.'

'Nearly fifty thousand,' she reminded him.

They were in the study at home. Henry was just back from a trip to London, ostensibly to check on some new items in their stock, but she knew better than that for his clothes reeked of her perfume. It did not matter much any more. The fact that they – or rather Henry – had lost such a lot of money did not matter either. Nothing mattered in life except your health because if you were fit and well you could cope with whatever life threw at you. Whereas once upon a time she would have been devastated by such a huge loss, she now found herself coldly detached from it.

And from her husband.

That day, at the hospital, when the results were through – and it was indeed just a cyst and nothing to worry about – Paula had taken her out for lunch and, with both of them in high spirits, what a jolly occasion that had been. It was as if their friendship had slipped into a different sphere; the superficial things no longer mattered. They got a little tipsy, the two of them, Paula deciding she had a liking for white wine and ordering them a bottle, which they consumed. Afterwards, going back to Paula's where they had left the car, she was in no fit state to drive and she stayed overnight. If Alan was surprised to see her when he got home he did not show it, although she heard whispered voices in the kitchen and guessed that Paula was telling him the reason why she was here.

She never intended to be alone with him that evening but Paula was called urgently next door to Alice's, so the two of them found themselves cosily sitting by the fire.

'Thanks for letting me stay.'

'No problem. I can't have you driving when you've had a few drinks.' He smiled. 'How many did Paula have? I haven't seen her looking like that for a long time. She doesn't usually let herself go.'

'I suppose she's told you about today?' she said.

He nodded. 'I'm glad for you. Thank God you're all right. Henry should have gone with you.'

'Henry doesn't know.'

'Why not? If it was Paula she would have told me.'

'We're different from you two,' she said, irritated suddenly. 'Surely you know that by now.'

'I do. I know it's not my business to interfere....'

'It isn't.'

'What's he playing at? You know, Eleanor, if you were married to me I wouldn't be looking at other women.'

She absorbed that comment, tucking it away, but not drawing attention to it. 'Has Paula been talking to you? Because she has no right to do that. What we talked about was confidential. I didn't mean for her to tell you.'

'Paula hasn't said a word. Henry has, though.'

Of course. He would brag about it, man to man, brag about all the women he had had, brag because he thought he had got away with it and that his poor wife knew nothing. It was so humiliating and so like him.

'Eleanor ...' Alan did not move from his chair, made no move towards her at all even though she so wanted him to. She wanted to be held close, to snuggle into him, to be told that he loved her. Henry had told her he loved her a million times but he did not mean it and although this man was never going to say it, he had no need to, for she saw in his eyes what he was not saying. 'I wouldn't hurt Paula for the world,' he went on, emphasizing it as if it needed to be emphasized.

'Don't say another word.'

The door opened and closed and Paula came through, shaking her head.

'It's over,' she said with a smile. 'We've found it. It was hiding in the shed under a pile of stuff. Alice was at her wits' end. The number of times I've had to help her look for that cat.' She looked at them, from one to the other, and Eleanor imagined the guilt in the room was palpable, but, if she knew, Paula did not acknowledge it as Alan got up to put more coal on the fire.

Henry was away at the time of her hospital visit so he had no idea what she had done. She had not told him about finding the lump in her breast. She did not tell him that she had a hospital appointment and she did not bother to tell him when it was all over.

She was done with Henry.

Looking at him as he sat at the desk trying to worm his way out of this situation, she was disgusted that he thought she knew so little about the inner workings of the business that he could pull the wool over her eyes. She knew exactly what he had done and she was almost annoyed that he had, as usual, got away with it.

She had been doing a lot of thinking lately and in spite of all the advice given to her, it was her decision alone as to what was going to happen next. She could carry on as usual, as she had been doing for years and years, or she could finally draw a line under all this.

'Don't worry about it,' Henry said, trying what she supposed he imagined was his winning smile. 'A minor hiccup, that's all and we'll soon put it behind us. We need to replenish the stock, though, so I think we ought to think about another Continental trip. I've had a request for some pretty specific items from the designer for a celebrity client.' He paused. 'Aren't you going to ask who it is?'

'I don't care.'

'Suit yourself, but we're talking megabucks here for his London pad. How about we get across to France next weekend?'

'Next week is no good. I've been talking to Paula and she has invited me for a spa weekend at a hotel near Bristol. It will be just the two of us and it's her treat. She insists.'

'She's treating you? What's up with you two? The tables have turned,' he sneered. 'Who does she think she is? Just because she's got money now she thinks she's something she isn't. Bloody spa hotel? She'll never have class no matter how hard she tries. And what's this I hear about amateur dramatics? Does she seriously think she can act, a woman like her?'

'I think she can act rather well. For instance I had absolutely no idea when we had lunch at that restaurant in Venice that you were groping her under the table. She never gave that away because she did not want to make a scene. She acted perfectly normally. You bastard, Henry.'

'Groping?' His face took on a puce colour. 'What's she on about?'

'Don't bother to deny it.' She was weary of him and his excuses. 'You were groping her, stroking her leg, and that's that. I believe her.'

'She was flirting.' He sounded defensive now. 'She was showing off her boobs in that frock.'

'It was nearly 90 degrees, for heaven's sake. And it was a very pretty frock if I recall. You shouldn't have been looking, but then you can't help that, can you? You just can't help it.' Her voice shook and she stopped as she caught the quick glance he shot at her. She was not going to cry. She was not going to cry at this late stage. Henry would love that. He would be all over her in seconds. 'She wouldn't play your game, would she, Henry?' Eleanor smiled a little. 'And that really rattles you, doesn't it? You think you can have any woman who takes your fancy and you can't. You can't have Paula for one.'

'Talk sense. Who wants her? If she was any shorter she'd be—'

'Shut up, Henry. I shall be going away on Friday with Paula and when I get back I expect you to be gone.'

'Gone where? What the hell are you talking about?'

'I'm leaving you,' she said. 'I've made up my mind so there's no point in arguing about it. I shall stay here and you can go and live with your current lady. After all I'm sure you have been comfortable recently when you stayed in her rather splendid apartment in London. She did well, didn't she? If you are going to marry a millionaire, marrying an elderly one with a heart problem seems ideal. Does the grieving widow think you're an adequate substitute? Perhaps she will change her mind when she finds out you have just lost fifty thousand pounds.'

'How do you know all this?' He had quietened, unable to hide his surprise. She could almost see his mind ticking over as he considered whether or not to deny it and then, having decided, she saw him smile. 'She's a hell of a lot warmer than you, my darling. You were a cold fish at the beginning and you've never warmed up. Making love to you is like making love to a mermaid. You've got the top half, I'll grant you that, but below ...'

'Don't be disgusting.' She spat out the words. 'If I had been with a man who loved me, who truly loved me, it would have been different, believe me.' She thought about the look Alan had given her, thought about him holding her hand, knew that, in another world, at another time, if he had never met

Paula, things might have been different.

'You fancy old Al, don't you?' he said with a laugh, reading her mind. 'Good God, I don't believe it. I caught the two of you holding hands and looking like lovesick teenagers when we were on holiday. If I were to mention that to Paula, it wouldn't half cause a few problems, wouldn't it?'

She had turned away with her back to him, and at those words she closed her eyes a moment as her heart pounded. And then, drawing on all her resources, she spun to face him and looked him straight in the eye. 'I don't know where you get that ridiculous idea from. Why on earth would I ever consider a man like Alan? It's preposterous, darling, but I suppose at the moment you can be forgiven for coming out with daft statements. I've caught you on the hop, haven't I? Can you imagine for one moment that I would give a man like Alan a second glance?'

She caught the hesitation and held his gaze and he was the first to look away.

'No, of course not,' he muttered gracelessly. 'Bloody stupid idea.'

'I've packed your things,' she told him. 'Your cases are up in the bedroom. You can return at any point if there's something you have forgotten but I shall be seeing my solicitor before long. I'm not in a terrible rush because I need to make sure I'm doing the right thing, but I take it you will not be contesting it when I do get round to it? To a divorce, that is.'

'What about the house and the business?' he asked at last, not quite looking at her. His voice was terse but calm. 'We have things to tie up. You can't just cut me loose like this. I'm entitled to things.'

'And so am I. I am sure we will come to an amicable arrangement. And now, if you'll excuse me, Henry, I need to get on with my packing for the weekend.'

Not only did she need to get on with the packing, she

reflected as she left him sitting there at his desk, stunned into silence, she needed now to get on with the rest of her life.

Time was precious and you had to make the most of every single minute.

Chapter Twenty-Three

PAULA WAS THRILLED when she passed her driving test. Why on earth had she waited so long to get a licence? Alan had never encouraged it, which was odd, but perhaps he enjoyed her being so dependent on him, an uncomfortable thought that niggled at her. He professed to be pleased when she passed, but she knew him well enough to know that he was not that pleased.

It was something she ought to have done years ago and she had proved to be a natural, having only the minimum of lessons before being put in for the test, which she passed first time. Maybe it was something to do with sitting beside Alan and observing him – subconsciously maybe – so that when it came to it, she half-knew all the things she needed to do and more importantly the things she must not do.

She had treated herself to a small car and it was so liberating to go off in it on her own that, coupled with everything else that had happened over the last few months, she felt like a new woman. She and Eleanor were friends now, proper friends, and it was all that business with the health scare that had done that, for all the veneer had been stripped away then and she had seen the real Eleanor underneath it. And now Eleanor had finally rid herself of Henry, which was a surprise because she had half-expected Eleanor to forgive him yet again.

Christmas was come and gone and they had got through it, although Henry not being around had made it tricky. It had been a mixed blessing, though, in a way because trying to keep Eleanor on an up-note and stop her thinking about her absent spouse had meant that she had not had as much time to think about Lucy, and next Christmas there would be a grandchild to spoil to make things even better.

Now it was spring and driving was no longer treacherous, which was a relief because Alan had driven her mad going on and on about icy roads and the perils of winter driving. He was such a fusspot and oddly nervous about her driving, refusing to let her drive when they were together in his car and never setting foot as a passenger in her car. Every time she went out in it, he wanted to know exactly where she was going and then she suffered a lecture about the difficulties of the route and what she must avoid.

She listened dutifully and promptly ignored him, choosing perversely to go by the route he did not recommend just for the sheer hell of it. She might be a new driver, but she reckoned she was competent enough to face whatever the roads and the road conditions and other road users might throw at her.

She had a very minor role in the Amateur Dramatic Society's midsummer musical production but she was the new girl so it was the best she could expect and she was no singer so she was being kept in the chorus as she should be. But she was still going to be there on stage and she was looking forward to it so much and enjoying going to the rehearsals and meeting like-minded people. She wished she could persuade Alan to join too because he had a good singing voice but he was not yet ready to do that so she was not pushing him.

She knew she had changed recently and Alan did not quite like it. He had not actually said as much, but after all this time she knew what he was thinking. He liked her as she was, as she used to be, and if things were a little strained between them these days, that was the downside of all this.

People changed.

Today she had waited for the school traffic to clear before setting out for Cornwall. There were several choices that would all lead her to Eleanor's house but she was taking the scenic route because it was a lovely morning and this road would be quieter. Alan had recommended that she concentrate purely on the driving until she was more experienced and that meant no listening to the radio or a CD.

But she was not only listening to a brand-new CD but singing along with it too as she neared the steep dip towards the river and the boundary bridge. She had spoken on the phone to Eleanor yesterday and she had booked them a table for lunch. Unlike Eleanor, Paula would not drink alcohol, not while driving, but she could take or leave wine so that was not a problem. This morning she was wearing a new outfit from a shop that specialized in petite clothes; expensive but beautiful clothes and she felt good, her hair long enough now to wear up if she wanted, which made it much more versatile.

Honeysuckle Cottage was hidden by the summer foliage of the trees but she stole a glance towards it. Nicola was expecting baby soon and they were all on a high waiting for it to arrive. They had said at first they did not want to know the sex but had changed their mind and now they knew that it was to be a girl, Clementine. Paula was working on the little nursery quilt at her quilting classes and it was coming along nicely.

On the way back this afternoon she might have time to pop by Tall Trees and pay a visit to her daughter-in-law and see how she was faring now that she was nearing the end of her pregnancy.

She checked her speed, slowed a fraction as she approached the next bend and it was then that something ran across the road, a cat, a ginger cat, and she braked and swerved because she could not run a cat over, not deliberately.

But she was still an inexperienced driver – as Alan had been at pains to tell her – and she could not correct the swerve and the car crashed through the barrier and, in a heartbeat, rocketed downwards towards the river.

Chapter Twenty-Four

THE FORECAST FOR the weekend was good and as a family they were taking advantage of it, meeting in the Green Parrot before taking the ferry across the estuary to Padstow. The tide was in, which meant they could not walk along the beach, but then family walks were impossible these days, what with the baby and the pushchair and Paula being in no fit state for walking any distance.

Eleanor was first in the café with Paula and Alan next to arrive. There had been a text from Nicola to say they were on their way and would be with them shortly.

'It's good to see you up and about,' Eleanor said as Paula lowered herself carefully into a chair with Alan hovering fussily behind her, taking the stick and hanging it on the back of the chair. Following the accident, the greatest damage had been to the legs and it had been an anxious few weeks, but the long-term prognosis was good.

'She's worried she's going to be shorter,' Alan said, taking a seat too and ordering drinks from the waitress. 'And she can't afford to lose an inch.'

They all laughed.

'You'll just have to wear higher heels,' Eleanor said. 'Once you get properly back on your feet, that is.' She rooted in the bag at her feet, showing them the sweet little dress she had bought Clemmie.

'You two will end up with the world's most spoilt grandchild,' Alan told them, shaking his head in disbelief. 'Paula's as bad as you. She's finished the quilt.'

'Have you? That is marvellous.'

'I'll show it you in a minute. It's in the car,' Paula said. 'It was a blessing because it gave me something to do all this time while I've been sitting around getting better.'

'And that's all that matters,' Alan said, reaching for her hand and briefly squeezing it. 'In the end, that's all that matters, isn't it, Eleanor? I could have lost her that day and I don't know what I would do without her.' He looked at Eleanor, a very direct look, and she knew what it meant. There were so many things that would forever remain unspoken between her and Alan. 'She was so lucky to walk away,' he added.

'I didn't walk away,' Paula said with a shudder. 'I was trapped by my legs.'

Eleanor looked out at the estuary, thinking momentarily about Henry, but quickly dismissing that thought and thinking instead about Clementine, who was by far the prettiest baby this side of the Atlantic. Looking across at Paula and Alan she knew that there had been yet another shift in their relationship, the accident denting Paula's newly discovered confidence so that they were very nearly back to square one.

Alan was happier now that Paula was once again fairly dependent on him and Paula seemed content too to settle once more into her familiar role. That new confidence, though, might be dented but it was not going to be squashed completely and Eleanor would make sure of that. She liked the new, improved, more confident Paula and she treasured their friendship more than ever now that Henry was gone.

Looking out of the window, she saw a harassed-looking Nicola – brand-new mum written all over her – heading their way, Matthew carrying the baby in a sling. They had that look of proud new parents and she in turn was proud of her daughter, who was rapidly learning the ropes of motherhood, those silken ties that bind you together for life.

'Here they are,' she pointed out to Paula, who had her back to them. 'Matthew's wearing the sling.'

'I can't wait to see her. I haven't seen her since last week,' Paula said, meaning Clemmie of course, and then, speaking quickly, before Alan reappeared from his loo visit: 'He thinks all this has put me off driving but it's not. I'm getting another car and I'll be back behind that wheel before you know it.'

'Good for you.' Eleanor saw the sparkle in her eyes and it was a relief to see it, for it had disappeared for a while following the accident.

'Don't say anything to Alan yet,' she muttered. 'I'll have to break it to him gently. He'll kick up a fuss but I'm determined.'

'I won't say a thing,' she promised.

It was sweet of Paula to trust her to keep a secret.

But then, she was very good at keeping secrets.